19|11

On Loki's Side

a book by

Alvis Kent

On Loki's Side © 2021 by Alvis Kent.

First Edition

ISBN: 9798501276178

Foreword

This book is for those who have used
their wit and wisdom to break free from
the chains of a largely Christian world.
Those of us who, much like Loki, have
broken the chains that bind us, now
seek to make a new world from our own
Ragnarok. The Good Lord Ing-Freyr is
said to loosen the bonds of men, and he
is a lover of plentitude and pleasure. So
also is Loki a lover of pleasure, and I
hope it pleases the reader to take in
what's written here, and think, because
this is first and foremost a book of
thinking. I hope that it will change your
outlook on Loki, and better your life.

Now shalt thou choose,
Since choice thou hast,
Hero 'neath shining helm,
To speak or stay silent,
All ill is spilled before you.

-- Sigrdrifumal 20

Table of Contents

RAIDHO   1

THURISAZ   12

WUNJO   30

ELHAZ   51

HAGALAZ   66

DAGAZ   89

OTHALA   102

PERTHRO   114

Introduction

Naglfar nears completion, but not to worry; it's always been nearly complete. The archetypal ghost-ship sails, just as Ragnarok is fought, within us each day. A whole cosmos of characters – gods & goddesses, dwarves & alfar, worms & roosters, frost & fire giants – exists in the spirit of each of us and Ragnarok will rage as long as they're at odds with one another. The leaf Age can never commence – Life & Lust for Life can never reach fruition – until psychological equilibrium is achieved.

Heathenism, Odinism, Asatru, whatever you choose to call it, is a natural religion, if it could be brought so low as to be called a religion. It's the way things are, not the way some may only wish they could be. This way isn't something which had to be revealed to some chosen few. It's apparent everywhere, if only you've got the capacity to see. There are no holy books, in the traditional sense of the phrase. There's no canon; no dogma. It's a living thing. What lore we have is the vision of me, divinely inspired by a force which is available to all, and therefore, any vision of the source of that inspiration – that Wode – is legitimate, regardless of its age, or antiquity. New additions – and in a living thing, there must be new life – whether in the form of myth, research, production, culture, or art, are brush strokes upon the masterpiece that is the Folk Soul, stitches in the tapestry of wyrd, and freshly sprouted chutes on this ever-changing, living thing that is human perception of universal truth.

Joseph Campbell and Carl Jung, both experts in comparative mythology, tell us that human understanding depends upon apprehension of pairs of opposites, but they add, these binary pairs are two parts of a whole. It's the whole we recognize as holy, not one side or the other.

Jung says "Nothing can exist without its opposite; the two were one in the beginning and will be one again in the end" (Four Archetypes. Princeton University Press, NJ. 1959).

The dualism of popular myth is the source of our present day disharmony, as a people, a species and as individuals. Both Jung and Campbell knew the cure for this spiritual disease. They'd learned it from dreams; their own, personal dreams and the collective dreams we share in myth. The disease, they said, is a division of the Self into a pair of opposites. Jung called the hidden fellow the Shadow, or the Aliquem Alium Internum – 'a certain other one, within'. The Self, he defined as the union of these opposites into a single being. He called this a unification process Integration. In order to realize one's full potential, he, or she, must make an effort to face this Shadow self and come to terms with it (Jung, '59).

The old myths can be likened to onions – savory, and sometimes musty – in that they're layered, and almost infinitely so. That's the meaning of esotericism; that the meaning behind these stories can be superficial and beneath the surface is layer after layer of meaning, in their relation to physical phenomena, historical events and personalities, personal and collective psychological components, social mechanisms and outright mysteries. They're both signs and symbols. Yes; they contain signs and symbols, as well as being signs and symbols themselves.

Campbell differentiates between the two, pointing out that signs direct our attention to easily understood ideas, like a stop sign tells us to stop and a question mark signifies that a question has been posed. A symbol, on the other hand is something which stands in for an inarticulable truth. The heart symbol represents love, but what is love? A rune is a symbol which represents an abstraction – Indefinite. Infinite. Out myths contain signs, like that of a fable, with definite moral lessons, and symbols, which stand in as representatives for things like inspiration and friendship, which are more difficult to define (Joseph Campbell, Flight of the Wild Gander).

This story was written with these facts in mind and while some may revolt against the idea of adding some apocryphal fiction to the existing lore, that doesn't change the fact that it was inspired by the same sense of awe experienced by our ancestors of a thousand, or more, years ago. I don't flatter myself with the notion of being their equal, or even comparable to contemporary myth-makers like Tolkien, but, at least, I believe my attempt was a plausible mimicry. If you refuse to believe anything can be added to the narrative – in spite of the fact that each day brings a new addition – this story can still serve the purpose of guiding one through the proper digestion of what you likely believe is the approved canon.

One layer of this neo-myth, let's call it, was meant to fill a gap in that narrative. We know, from Lokasenna (verse 9), that Odin and Loki are oath bound to one another, but the details of that youthful bond are lost. So here we have a possible version of such a friendship. It was a convenient place to tell a meaningful story which wouldn't impede upon what came before and after – if in fact we could coherently chronicle the plot in Rydbergian fashion – and a good opportunity to attempt a better understanding of the relationship between the figure of Odin and Loki.

This begs the question, who, or what, are Odin and Loki? They aren't, we can say with confidence, God and the Devil, although some parallels could be drawn between the two pairs. Normally, as a holistic religion, we try to refrain from demonizing, or idealizing, things into absolutely evil or perfect good. In the case of the present allegory, Odin and Loki represent aspects of the psyche of every living person. Everyone. The archetypal images of what they represent in the human consciousness (and unconscious) are universal, though their individual identifying attributes – their names, clothing, weapons and attendants – are specific to the Northern European collective unconscious and are exclusives.

Campbell says "Just as we have a physical body that we share with each other, so that we can respond similarly to the same smells, so also we have a spiritual consciousness that is responding to comparable signals, and the whole concept of the archetypes of the human psyche is based on the notion that the human brain, in the human sympathetic nervous system, there are structures that create a readiness to respond to certain signals. These are shared by all humanity, with variations individually, but essentially pretty close along the line." (Pathways to bliss: Mythology and Personal Transformation, New World Library. Novato CA, 2004).

The idea that all of our deities and all of the characters of the lore are components of our individual and collective psyches is harnessed here to flesh out Jung's process of Shadow Integration.

Like Freud, Jung compartmentalized the psyche into different levels of consciousness and identity. Freud's version was layered from the Superego, which Campbell describes as the 'I must not' factory, programmed into us by society, down to the Ego, described as the superficial awareness of the deep, unknown Self and as a "function which relates you to reality in terms of your personal judgment, not the judgments you have been taught to make, but the judgments that you do make." Lower still is the Id, which Campbell called the "I want" machine, synonymous with our limbic instincts, linking it with Jung's archetypes.

The Superego, being programmed over time through experience, is the product of the Prefrontal Cortex – the last brain region to fully mature and the seat of higher order consciousness and advanced moral reasoning. The Ego is another Cortical function, though this level of consciousness is shared with the rest of the primate family and only mistakenly perceived as chief amongst the litter of little minds in our heads. The Id is the product of the lower level, unconscious mind – our mammalian and reptilian instincts. What we know as mind is an interaction between all of these levels: Consciousness, Subconsciousness and Unconsciousness.

Jung recognized this as well, but being the mystic and mythologist that he was, added some relevant concepts to the paradigm. Above the level of consciousness, again, is the Ego, but mirroring the Ego exactly, below the level of consciousness, is the Shadow. The Shadow doesn't comprise the whole of the unconscious: it's just the Alter Ego.

Campbell said "[The Shadow is] that which you won't look at abut yourself. Like Freud's unconscious it is repressed recollections and potentialities…In the myths the Shadow is represented as the monster that has to be overcome (the dragon). It is the dark thing that comes up from the abyss and confronts you the minute you begin moving down into the unconscious…The Shadow is that part of you that you don't know is there. Your friends see it, however, and it's also why some people don't like you…You should find a way to realize your Shadow somehow." (Campbell, '04).

Compare this with Jung's statement: "As we know, a complex can really be overcome only if it's lived out to the full. In other words, if we are to develop further we have to draw to us and drink down the very dregs what, because of our complexes, we have held at a distance." (Jung, '59)

In other words, we have to face our shadow in order to actualize what Jung called the self, a union of opposites, and realize our potential. This united whole can be seen in the myth of the World Tree, which contains so many binary pairs, but is, itself, the thing which ties them all together. No wonder then, it's described as Odin's horse – Yggdrasil – and he, as the archetypal spirit traveler, driven to seek out the unknown and the hidden, courageous enough to face the uncomfortable realities and make peace with them, or destroy them if need be. In this story, which takes place at the beginning of his life of wandering, he confronts his own Shadow in the person of Loki and must decide whether to continue repressing him, or to 'drink down the dregs', as it were.

Jung says "The transformation processes strive to approximate them to one another, but our consciousness is aware of resistances, because the other person seems strange and uncanny, and because we cannot get accustomed to the idea that we are not absolute master in our own house. We should prefer to be always 'I' and nothing else. But we are confronted with that inner friend, or foe, and whether he is our friend or our foe depends on ourselves." (Jung, '59)

Deeper still, within the unconscious, Jung placed the archetypes. As Campbell has been quoted, touching upon their nature, Jung equated them to the instincts, at the very same level as Freud's Id, albeit much more complex and diverse and minus the almost complete preoccupation with sex Freud was so well known for. They're the accumulated instincts, stored within the collective unconscious, that have provided mankind with a distinct survival advantage since our earliest stages of evolution. The implications of that idea are that people aren't the only creatures whose psyches are home to archetypes; we're just the only ones who have dredged them up from the depths and created mythologies about them, dressing them in costumes and providing them with personalities specific to our own ethnic identities and Egos.

Jung said "In themselves, archetypal images are among the highest values in the human psyche; they have peopled the heavens of all races from time immemorial." (Jung, '59).

This brings these lowest levels of instinctual unconsciousness up to the heights of human awareness, thus uniting yet another pair of opposites. These instincts can be animalistic and chaotic, as well as the arbiters of order and civilization.

While in this story Odin faces his shadow and the archetypes of his own unconscious, in our own cases Odin and Loki are only a couple of archetypes of the many hidden in the depths and we must discover the nature of our own shadow self.

Jung goes on to say "A Primordial image is determined as to its content only when it has become conscious and is therefore filled out with the material of conscious experience. Its form, however,…might perhaps be compared to the axial system of a crystal, which, as it were, performs the crystalline structure in the mother liquid, although it has no material existence on its own…The representations themselves are not inherited, only the forms, and in that respect they correspond in every way to the instincts, which are also determined in form only." (Jung, '59).

So as Odin, here, and we, in our own spiritual quests, dive down into the unconscious and face these 'primordial images', we're saddled with the burden of bringing them back to the surface of reason and fashioning them into comprehensible characters. Before they're brought into the light of reason, they remain amorphous, but likewise, having faced them, we expand our frames of reference, enlarge our personalities and increase our levels of consciousness. It's really a heroic deed. That's why this story, as well as our own quests of self-discovery, follow the outline of what Campbell called The Hero's Journey.

It's through the simple act of facing these hidden repressions and complexes that we're able to bring them up from the depths of the unconscious to the level of the Ego, thereby incorporating them into who we see ourselves as – integrating them into the Self – as opposed to allowing them to remain the monsters under the bed who you'd rather avoid thinking about. We tend to fear the unknown and the misunderstood, while after illuminating these things, we realize there was never anything to fear because they are actually only parts of ourselves. The slaying of the dragon doesn't destroy its power; it's only subsumed into the Self as was the case when Sigurd ate Fafnir's heart.

Campbell's' Hero's Journey follows a certain pattern. Having studied the myths of many cultures throughout the world and across the millennia he was able to generalize upon the thread of these myths based upon their common elements. Because of the shared psychology of humankind, it's safe to say these parallels resemble the neural pathways which transmit that we know as our unique human attributes as opposed to those we share with chimps and wolves.

Campbell summarizes the Hero's Journey, saying "The basic story of the Hero's Journey involves giving up where you are, going into the realm of adventure, coming to some kind of symbolically rendered realization, then returning to the field of normal life." (Campbell, '04)

When we superimpose this outline over many of our myths we can see how true it is. This summary only provides some proof for the applicability of Campbell's observation, whereas the details of each stage of the journey help us come to a better understanding of what the myths mean.

The first stage of the journey is the call to adventure, in which the hero is led away from where he, or she, is, or is driven out. The hero must decide whether to answer the call or ignore it. Campbell says "unfortunately, those who choose to refuse the call don't have a life. Either they die, or in trying to lead more mundane lives, they exist as nonentities, what T.S. Eliot called 'hollowmen'." (Campbell, '04)

The second stage, having left the sphere of mundane life, the hero comes into contact with a guide, or a helper of some kind, who offers assistance as a means to success. This can be seen in the legend of Svipdag, as he receives 'Nine Spells', from his temporarily resurrected mother, Groa, which are to aid him along the way (Svipdagsmal) and in the present story, Odin's helper is his own Alter Ego, Loki.

The next stage is a test, or trial, or a series of them. The deeper into the unknown the hero goes, the more difficult and threatening his journey becomes.

Campbell describes this phase as "...the repression system you have to pass through," confronting the various elements of your, as of yet, unintegrated psychological components: the Shadow, Anima/Animus, archetypes, vices and virtues.

The final phase of the journey is the return and the crossing of the Threshold back into mundane experience. This, like the call to Adventure, is accompanied by its own hazards. Not only does the other World not always want the hero to escape with its secrets, the mundane isn't always receptive to the perceived treasures the hero has recovered from the depths. Many items the shamanic spirit-traveler becomes an outcast from regular society and his perspective is so unalterably shifted, he can no longer fit into his former role or the status quo. (Campbell, The Hero with a thousand faces, Princeton University Press, NJ. 1949).

The Sigurd cycle – from whichever source you get it – is an almost perfect example of the Hero's journey. Campbell refers to it, saying "Siegfried and Fafnir, the dragon that he kills – the typical dragon-killing deed of the hero crossing the threshold. He and the dragon are opposites, but it's only when he has tasted the dragon's blood and integrated the dragon character in himself that he hears the birds sing and knows what their song is saying. You don't get in touch with the nature force which includes both you and the other until you have accepted as part and parcel of yourself the formerly excluded part, that which was seen to be other." (Campbell, '04).

As I've mentioned, myths, this story included, are multidimensional, so in addition to all the psychobabble between the lines, there are some very basic moral imperatives easily seen on the surface. These include the acceptance of others, and yourself, in spite of potentially repulsive character flaws through understanding. When we face our own flaws through the integration process it becomes much easier to bear the flaws of others – and makes us hypocrites when we fail to do so. Also herein is expressed a gratitude for family and a place to call home. So often we take these people and places for granted while we have them and only realize their value after we've lost, or forfeited them. The loss is almost justified in the realization though, which is arguably as valuable as the frith – the force represented by Wunjo – itself. Another superficial element here is the necessary reciprocity of friendships and familial relationships. The force represented by Gebo is a common element throughout.

In spite of the fairly juvenile plot, the subtext should provide enough depth to inspire some consideration from even a mature reader. At least, I hope it may. As I've said, being provided this insider's guide – this road map – the story at hand can be used as a tool for the exploration of the rest of the myths within the lore with the Self as a focal point. There are worlds within us, each populated by a host of characters. Every god and ghoul in our lore is an aspect of the Self, in addition to being sign posts and symbols throughout the physical, in space and time.

These mythos are timeless and therefore they each take place within us eternally and on a daily basis. That's why they're so important. Our inner Ragnaroks and Leaf Ages are what connect us to the spirit of our own people, to humankind as a whole, and most importantly the whole of ourselves. They're what provide us with a guide on our own hero's journeys so we aren't left to navigate a disordered cosmos alone, rudderless and without a wind to fill our sails. It's through the integration process we forestall the embarkation of Naglfar by transforming it into Skithblathnir. (Grimnismal).

On Loki's Side

By Alvis Kent

Young was I once and went alone
And wandering lost my way
When a friend I found I felt me rich
Man is cheered by man

--Havamal 47

With a friend a man should be friends ever
And pay back gift for gift
Laughter for laughter he learn to give
And eke lessing for lies

-- Havamal 42

"How did it come to this?" Odin thinks to himself."

"From this seat. Through my eye, I've seen so much. The sun is setting; it seems like she is always setting these days. It's twilight, the twilight of time."

The grizzled old god clenches his powerful fist around the shaft of his spear.

"Would you like something to drink dear?" a comforting voice calls.

'Yes. Mead." He sais distractedly.

"Frigga" he thinks, "We've grown old".

A cup appears before him and he suffers a smile to his caring wife.

"Wine" he says to himself as he looks at the cup. "It's been wine alone for so long. Geri. Freki. You do all my eating for me now, don't you?" he sais to the two huge wolves at his feet. Their fur is graying around their shouts.

"I think I saw old Freki limping. How long ago we met…Loki" Odin mouths the name and frowns.

"I'm sorry my old friend" he thinks as his gaze drifts through time and space to some distant, dark place. A snake writhes over Loki's face. Venom trickles down the rock he has been stretched across.

"We're not boys anymore" the one-eyed god whispers to Loki across an unfathomable distance.

"The sun was rising then. She always seemed to be rising…Ida plain"[1]. Odin's mind drifts once more."

"I was just a boy. I knew so little. A small lake hath but little sand.[2] What would I give to be back there? The bounds of my small world swaddling me like a babe."

Odin gives into his soul searching and peers through the eye he left in the well of Mimir.

Raidho

"Vili!" I hear my young voice call. "Will! I'm

My brother looked at me condescendingly. "No Odin. In fact, you and Ve ought to come with me. I found another fallen stone. I might need your help standing it back up."

I looked at the ground, trying to think of an excuse. "I can't. I'm gonna be gone all day, maybe longer. Can we try some other time?"

"I'll just figure a way to do it by myself then. Maybe Ve will still help. Where is he anyway? You seen him?"[2]

I just shrugged and walked away grumbling under my breath. "He never cooperates. Always does what he wants. Maybe Ve will go with me, but I doubt it."

I searched the long house, not a place to hang around all day. The thick, stone and turf walls, too busy holding up the heavy, soot-stained roof-beams to allow light through.

"This house…" I thought as I walked to the corner of the great room where my things were stored, "…So miserable".

Any other day I would have just grabbed my staff and wide-brimmed hat and taken off into the forest, but on this day I had planned to explore further than I'd ever gone before.

"We ought to know where it ends. We're gods, after all" I thought as I picked up my satchel. "Gods are supposed to know these things, not just hang around the house".

I held the bag and searched through my belongings intently.

"My horn. I might get thirsty". I stuffed it into the bag.

"What else? My knife." I carefully pulled the blade from its hiding place, admiring it as I did every time I held it.

"Stinger, forged in the fires of the Dark Elves". I repeated the story I'd been told when the knife was given to me.

"Might need to do some hunting, or trapping. A snare". I opened a small pouch at hand and untangled a long piece of cat-gut from within it and placed it, too, in the satchel.

"In the meantime" I thought as I stood, "I'll take enough meat for a day or two".

I walked to the larder and removed a hefty portion of salted boar's meat.

"You put up a fight, didn't you Long-Tusk?" I rhetorically asked the meat at I wrapped it in a piece of old linen.

"Considering the effort of hunting you, I'll enjoy eating your rump all the more".

Smiling, I stuffed this, as well, in my, then, full travel bag. Even for a boy of my youth, I was very resourceful, able to do things others my age hadn't yet thought to learn. My parents must have been very proud, proud to have had sons who broke the mold.

"Odin! Wode! Can you help me for a moment?" My mother's voice called from the next room.

"Coming Mother" I said, then thought to myself "she must be spinning yarn, needs me to lift a whorl or something".

I dutifully went to her.

"Son, will you change the whorl on the spinning wheel?" she asked, as predicted.

I lifted the obscenely large stone pulley and fitted it on the contraption.

"Is that all Mother?"

"Yes my boy".

She looked me up and down. "Where are you off to?"

"The Ironwood. Exploring". I said briefly, not wanting to inspire too much curiosity in her.

"Well, don't wander off too far. I know how you are. In fact, why don't you take one of your brothers with you so you're not alone."

"Vili's busy" I said. "I'll ask Ve though."

"Okay Wode; be careful."

I dashed from the house, my satchel strapped to my back, hat securely fitted to my head and my long walking stick in hand, my haste, and effort in avoiding any further questions or demands from the house's inhabitants.

At the gate to the inner garth I yelled "Ve!...Ve!"

I stopped, listening intently for a response. Nothing.

"Always off somewhere daydreaming" I thought as I continued on down the well-trodden path into the surrounding pasture.

Hills rose lazily in the distance, obscuring my line of sight, not that I needed to see it to know what was there. I'd explored all of that land so extensively, I knew every rock and what lied beneath it.

"There's nothing here" I said aloud. "I hate this boring place"

And then, BOOM! a thunderous noise shook the ground, interrupting my self-pity.

"What the…" I said as I started running excitedly toward the commotion, hoping to find something worth seeing.

I created the slope and the only word that came to mind was "Giants." I just looked on disgustedly at the cause of the noise.

"Aesir!" The giant bellowed from stop a huge, fallen stone. He pointed toward the remaining stones still standing in a monumental circle.

"Plenty more to topple. The fun's not all been had."

"Wouldn't call that fun, Giant" I snarled. "Those stones are there for a reason."

"And what reason would that be, Odin?"[3]

"I don't know, but somebody put them there and you're messing them up, for what?"

"For fun, that's what. If you don't want to help, why don't' you just keep on walking."

"I ought to teach you some respect" I said threateningly, "but I don't have time to waste trying to teach a senseless beast virtue."[4]

"Go on then, we'll both be better off."

At that, I forced myself to turn back toward my path.

"Ye gods, I hate those creatures" I thought to myself, trying desperately to make it to the forest before anything else unexpected delayed me.

"Where are you Ve? Always hidden in plain sight. I'll end up searching for him all day."

My pessimism proved false because only another hill over I stumbled upon him.

"Ve! I've been looking for you forever." I unceremoniously interrupted my brother's reverie. "What are you doing?"

"Watching the sky. What are you doing?" Ve fired back rhetorically.

"Why are you wasting your time staring off into space? There's nothing up there but blue eternity."

"Maybe there should be something there.[5] May be even that empty space should be appreciated from time to time. What do you think about that Wode? Why are you bothering me anyway?"

"I'm going to the Ironwood again.[6] I'm going to find where it comes out. You wanna come?"

My brother just closed his eyes and stretched out on the grass. "Nah, I'm good." He said dismissively. "Nothing out there but trouble. You probably should just stay around the house anyway. Mom might need your help."

I didn't even deign to respond before I walked away across the grassy plain.

Many times I had explored the Ironwood. As many times, I'd gone alone. It could be a forbidding place. The trees were ancient and huge. Their roots spread across the forest floor like a nest of snakes. The tree limbs were mighty and gnarled, hung with long ropes of creepy moss.

I still believed the Ironwood might stretch out forever, covering the rest of the world. Even that wouldn't have been beyond the bounds my mother had set for me. I had ventured deep, deep into it and had yet to find its end. The trees only grew larger, thicker and more frightening.

I'm not afraid" I would tell myself. "It's not scary at all."

Even at that age I always had a few tricks up my sleeve.

"Come what may, as long as I use my head. I can think myself out of most any situation" I told myself, and most of the time I actually could.

The Ironwood lay in the East, toward the rising sun. As I walked, I entertained myself speaking to the world around me in verse, as I still do from time to time.

"Why, dear Sunna" I said to the waxing sun, "do you sleep in the East, but never wander West?" You bound into the bright blue sky, eager to meet the morning. Then back to bed, before you test the bounds you could be soaring."

In that distant past, the morning of time, the sun had not yet learned to travel all the way across the sky. She rose from the West, only to return there after she had her fill of the day.[7]

"I thought to change that.

"You have much to learn Sunna, but not to worry; I'll show you the way" I assured her.

Young though I was, when I committed myself to a task, I intended to finish it, by any means. Even in those days, it seemed the more daunting a task might be, the more inclined to undertake it I became. I was, and remain, sort of stubborn in that way.

"Grass" I remember saying quietly, "what are you whispering down there? Barley? What song is that you're singing?"

The tall stalks which dotted the plain swayed in the wind, while the thick turf cushioned my footfalls. My boots tread the ground of my homelands, which radiated strength into me, but even so, unwanted thoughts once again invaded my mind.

"My brothers; always doing what they want to do and never a moment to share. Vili. Why is he so bossy? Can't he ever just get lost in something unknown? And Ve. Such a dreamer. Come back Ve" I said aloud and chuckled to myself.

Then my mind drifted again."

"Stupid giants; always destroying stuff. Never done anything worth. I don't think they're even capable of learning. Come to think of it, I've never learned anything from them either."[8]

"What am I doing?" I chastised myself, "Stay focused on the road ahead Wode."

I lapsed back into my conversation with the surrounding country.

"Oh Ironwood forest, how far have you spread? Have you come to the clearing to upend Sunna's bed? What lies beyond your writhing reaches? Is it mountains, or moors, badlands, or beaches?"[9]

Only a few more steps and my mind wandered again.

"Frightful Sunna, someday you will fare into the winds of the West if you dare. If there are thurses or beasts blocking your way then I lust for the battle and will live for the day."

My thoughts broke from their poetic musings at that, refocusing on this day's adventure.

"A trip into the far West will have to wait thought. Today I discover if there is a monster holding you back, rather than one impeding you."

The thought of a possible battle excited me, inspired me, and an irresistible smile stretched across my face, hurrying my feet to a near-run as the edge of the unending forest appeared over the crest of a low hillock.[10]

As I approached, the trees divided themselves from one huge, undifferentiated mob, into singular monoliths. Their shadows stretched toward me as Sunna was slowly consumed below their tops. The closer I walked, the darker the forest became, until it was difficult for me to tell whether it was still day, or night.

I paused for a moment, taking in the grandeur of the looming arbor, glancing back at the rolling, grassy hills of Ida Plain, and thinking ambivalently of home.

I have always felt more strongly drawn to wandering. I stepped into the dusky forest with a feeling of longing, but not longing for the familiarity of my garth, behind is safe walls. I felt, instead, a longing for the familiar thrill of the unknown which lay ahead.

I tread an old path, between, under and from the top of one root, to another, I used my staff to vault across the trickling bed of a shallow creek. I clambered up the face of a small stone cliff, as I had done so many times before. I moved quickly and with a sure foot. Although of the Ironwood, these were still my places.[11]

Deeper and deeper into the forest I flew like a stag, or a wolf; my imagination flew out ahead of me like a raven, seeking out the things and places I had yet to see in person. My mind flew with it. Those ravens, almost so real I could touch them. I flew ever faster into the wilderness of my spirit.

"Come on legs," I chided myself "haven't you got more speed within you? We've been down this path before. No need for tip-toing. Let's come to the end of this well known way so the journey can finally begin."

While I didn't know fully, I suspected that every step beyond the outer limits of my past wanderings would be one that would change the direction of my life. It was, and remains, the principle guiding my wyrd to this day. I still gaze at the horizon, wondering what may lie beyond. Has it changed? Are the forces of night gathering there?

Thurisaz

Just ahead I saw what had marked the extent of my last expedition I had taken notice that as I ventured deeper into the Ironwood, the terrain had become more and more rocky. I had also taken notice of the markings which appeared on some of the large boulders I passed. There were runes deeply carved and craftily placed, so as not to arouse the attention of the typical traveler. They struck me as being different than the symbols I had seen on the standing stones of the plain. These, deep in the woods, seemed unfriendly, though I hadn't yet learned to read them. All I could assume was that these runes indicated the presence of forces I had never before confronted, possibly hostile giants of a different sort than the breed I was accustomed to.[2]

There was one large stone teetering on the edge of a narrow chase.[3] Upon it was carved what I could only think of as a thorn. When I neared the stone, that image invaded my mind, so, listening to my intuition, I felt, rather than knew for certain, what the symbol meant.[4]

"There, beside the standing stone; a way across" I thought to myself as I projected my imagination ahead.[5]

There lay a large, flat rock, overhanging the breach, providing a point from which to jump.

"I'll mount here, then I can run and jump. There's clear spot on the other side for me to land. If I leap with all of my strength, I think I can make it."

Another part of my spirit tried to dissuade me.[6]

"You might not though. You might not be strong enough."

This naysayer showed me this version of my future, and in it I failed, my fingers gripping the edge of the cliff, nothingness beneath me, fear coursing through my veins.

"No" I told that coward. "We'll see, won't we?"

In spite of this lingering doubt, I mounted the slab. Removing my hat, I tucked it into my belt. I gripped my staff with white knuckles and bolted, managing three bounding strides before the edge of the overhang forced me to leap, at last.

I jumped as if my life depended on it and in this case, my life certainly did depend upon it. Soaring over the rift, I found that I never lost my presence of mind. In my brief moment of flight over the emptiness below, I wondered if those depths might descend all the way to Hel, the realm of the dead. This, of course, was a question to be answered at another time. For now, my focus was retrained upon the other side of the breach.

I came down fast, managing one more long, controlled stride, then another, before I noticed a large, slick-looking pile of brown poop directly under where my next step would fall. However fleet of foot I may have been back then, this I could not avoid. My boot squished down into the revolting mound, splattering smelliness up my pant-leg.

"Don't fail me Balance." I thought as my feet tried to find purchase.

"This isn't the time to show off Speed." I said as that part of me veered out of control. Neither my Balance, nor my Speed paid my wished any mind. They were preoccupied with their own. These two menaces grappled with one another, their wrestling match becoming a tangle, robbing me of any usefulness they might have otherwise provided.

I was thrown into an uncontrollable cartwheel, tumbling head over needs. The waste which was once only on my feet and legs was now evenly spread over most of my clothes and body. I felt hard, jagged rocks and gravel abusing me along the way before I came to an abrupt stop, my head nearly smashing a boulder to smithereens. I could be hard-headed, but in this department, the big rock had me beat. I saw stars for only a moment before all went dark and I was forced to take a midmorning nap there, covered in dooky, on the rocky floor of that unexplored wilderness.

I wasn't asleep for very long, but while I was out I dreamt of lightning coming from the clear blue sky, igniting the dry underbrush of the forest floor. In my dream the fire grew to engulf the surrounding trees, leaving me no choice but to try and beat back the flames for as long as I could.

"This battle, I cannot win" I thought to myself rhetorically. That familiar voice of doubt reassuring me.

"Stop fighting then" it said. "Just lie down and give up."

Those words tasted like poison in my mouth though.

"I must fight!" I yelled. "I have no choice."[7]

Just when I was certain that the end was upon me, I awoke with a start, a steam of drool running down my cheek into the dirt I lay in.

Through a blurry set of eyes I saw a real fire and believed, for a moment, that I might still be dreaming. This was no forest fire. It was only what appeared to be a small camp fire a good distance away from where I lay.[8]

The shock of my vision had me feeling a bit nervous though. I could hear my father's voice warning me of the dangers of unattended fires.

"Wode," he would begin, "all fires must be held in check. Even the world of fire, Musple, is held at bay by the ice world. A fire left to its own devices is greedy and will consume everything until there is nothing left, even for itself."

With this in mind I quickly sprang to my feet, only then realizing how hard I must have hit my head when keeping my balance proved to be more difficult than it should have been. Without much thought I picked up my staff and walked unsteadily toward the flame, rubbing the goose-egg on my head along the way. I stumbled forward, my walking-stick finally serving its intended purpose, and didn't notice that I wasn't gaining on the fire at all. Every step I took toward it seemed to push it away, as if it had sprouted legs and was purposefully running from me.

"Me head" I thought as I stumbled, but then the rest of the picture began to take shape. "What is this I'm covered in? Gods, it stinks. Smells like…ughh…cat poop."

Even now, after all these years, I've not found a more foul smell than the dung of a mountain lion.

The flame shifted quickly toward me, enough to catch my attention, then away again. When I looked up, I finally realized that the fire was as far away now as it had ever been. I knew something was amiss.

I stopped in my tracks to assess the situation. The fire sat still for a moment.

"Could it be a figment of my imagination?" I asked myself.

Blinking hard, I shook my head as if there were water in my ears. I was beginning to think more clearly now. I knew I was awake. All of my senses were active and after regaining my composure, highly alert. The fire, I decided, was as real as Sunna was bright.

I leapt into action, trying to get the better of the tricky little flame. As if it had been waiting for me to act, the flame moved with me, though much more swiftly this item, transporting itself fluidly, a good distance up the path.

I was not discouraged. I picked up my pace, committed to following the fire until it was subdued.

For quite some time I gained no ground, but finally I took notice of a rock ledge to my left. Assuming the fire would move in the opposite direction, I moved right. As predicted, the flame stayed ahead and started moving toward the rocky outcropping.

I pressed my advantage until I was sure the pesky fire could not jump the high embankment. Then, I changed my course, forcing the flame toward the wall of stone. I spied a tight little nook in the face of the cliff and sped my pursuit, unavoidably directing my quarry into it.

Apparently, before the fire realized what was happening, if it was keen enough to think about such things, it was cornered and I was stepping slowly toward it. The unfortunate flame had nowhere to go.

"I don't know what, or who, you are, my friend, but I intend to put an end to your troublemaking" I threatened the mischief-maker.

The flames increased their intensity as if to deter me from my promise. The tactic did not work.

I pounced, stomping at the edges of the fire until it was clearly being beaten back. I pulled my hat from my belt and was about to use it to smother what was left of the flames when the voice of what sounded like a young man began pleading with me.

"My friend! My friend! You said we were friends! Give me a break, whoever you are!"

Before I could finish extinguishing the fire, it transformed itself into a boy of about my age. His hair remained the same color as the flames from which he had been born. The boy's eyes were the vibrant color of green only seen in the leaves freshly sprouting from the crown of a springtime oak. Those eyes squinted and smiled, as if to say they knew something the rest of the world had yet to learn. Where I was thickly built, with strong arms and legs, this boy was thin and spindly, like the limbs which sprung from the same treetops his eyes had come from.[9]

At first, the boy lay on the ground defending himself from my onslaught, but when he changed form I couldn't help but be taken aback, giving him enough respite to gain his feet. He moved with a quickness which betrayed his frail appearance.

With much practice, I was able to deftly retrieve my knife from the bag at my side. I wasn't sure what sort of creature this was.

"Who are you," I shouted, "and what's your business here?"

The irony of this statement was lost on me then, but not Loki.

"My name is Loki," the boy said as he extended his hand for a shake, seeming not to notice the threatening looking knife pointed in his direction, "and the Ironwood is my home. I might more rightfully ask you the same questions, for it was you who hunted me where I had been living in peace". His tone didn't quite match the welcoming look on his face.

"I am Odin, son of Borr, who was the son of Buri, the first god. My mother's name is Bestla. I am from Ida Plain and I'm here to discover the limits of this forest." I nervously over explained, still not letting down my guard.

"Ooh, a pedigree" Loki said sarcastically, withdrawing his unshaken hand. "Well, then, it is

I, Loki, son of Farbauti, the son of Ymir, the first giant. My mother is Laufey and, as I've said, this," Loki waved his hand dramatically toward the surrounding forest, "is my home. It appears, Odin of Ida Plain, we are cousins, of a sort."

I cringed. It was true that my mother was of the line of Ymir, but that was unavoidable, since everybody, sparing my grandfather, Buri, came from that wretched old giant.

Ymir had a stranglehold on the world. He was responsible for the sun's shyness. He was the reason why the barley would only grow in clumps, scattered about the plain. Ymir, I understood, was the cause of everything holding me and my family back from prosperity.[10]

"That may be true, Loki Farbautison; giant," my disdain for giantkind dripping from that last word like an insult, "but the blood of my mother and her kindred is far more noble than you others who were born of Ymir's toe-jam".

Loki laughed a happy, genuine laugh. "That's a good one" he said, trying to catch his breath. "I suppose my kin did have a rather disgusting beginning, but at least we are far enough removed from him to have learned to bathe, while you and yours seem not to mind being filthy. What is it you've covered yourself in? It smells terrible."[11]

I had almost forgotten my tumble back at the chasm, having grown accustomed to the smell of the dung, but when Loki pointed it out to me it came back, forcing me to squinch up my nose in revulsion.

"I seem to have gotten myself into a mess one of the forest dwellers left on the floor of your home. At least where I come from we know the proper place to attend to such business."

Again, Loki belted out an infectious laugh and I couldn't help but allow myself to smile. This boy had a catching sense of humor. My defenses were broken. I let down my knife and after leaning my staff against the rock, extended my hand to return the handshake I'd denied moments before.

Loki met it and we finally shared a proper introduction.

"Nice to meet you, Loki of the Ironwood."

"And you, Odin Borson. I believe I must personally apologize for the accident you stumbled upon, I…" Loki paused as if trying to conjure some lie.

"I know of a fearsome and beautiful creature who is wont to leave such jewels on the doorstep of my home. I am sure he is aware of the hazards of the practice."

Loki withdrew his hand and gazed at it in disgust for a second before looking up at me with a smile and casually wiping his palm on the thigh of his britches.

"I know a place where you can clean yourself up, that is, if you are inclined toward such things. I'm unfamiliar with the customs of the plain. After that, I think I can help you accomplish your goal here. I happen to know just where the Ironwood ends and I believe you'll be surprised at the distance we'll have to travel."

Loki motioned at the ground, as if to point out to me that the path we must take lay under my feet. I realized I still had him cornered and as I made way for him to lead us on I thanked him.

"I'd be grateful for your hospitality, and yes," I felt the need to defend myself, "we do bathe."

"Have you made the journey to the edge of the forest often?" My enthusiasm betraying my childish excitement. "I imagine it is difficult and dangerous. You must be quite the woodsman."

Loki just looked back at me with a snarky smile as he led the way, only responding by saying, cryptically, "I wouldn't call it the 'far' edge."

I continued on, unphased. "How do you know the beast whose scat I slipped in was a male? I mean, does it have markings that tell you, or what?"

"Loki sniggered under his breath. "Let's just say I'm very familiar with this 'beast', as you call it."

"That's a very nice knife you've got there Odin." He said with a glance and an eye-roll, for those perceptive enough to notice.

I happened to be very perceptive and snapped to the fact that I was still gripping it. Embarrassed, I began to tuck it into my satchel.

"It was a gift from my grandfather, Bolthorn. One of your uncles, I believe. He said it was crafted by the dark elves, but I don't know much about them. It must be very old.[12]

I looked down at the knife, turning it over in my hand reflectively. It was silver and gold, inlayed with a host of indecipherable runes down the blade and along the hilt.

"It's meant to be thrown," I continued. "I've been practicing and I've gotten pretty good at it." I looked up just before dropping it in. "Do your want to see?"

"Sure", Loki brightened up a little, "that'd be great."

I pulled the knife back out and paused on the path to choose my target. My sight honed in on the trunk of a large pine tree. Loki stopped with me and stood smiling and squinting in his charming way.

I drew the sleek-looking knife back quickly over my shoulder, holding it by its smoothly wrought handle, and just as quickly, with the flick of my wrist, let loose. The knife flew toward the tree in a streak of shimmering light, almost too fast to be seen.

Loki surely heard it hum as it flew. When it struck the tree it embedded itself deeply, buzzing like the wings of a wasp in flight.

"That was quite impressive." He said before giving a mockingly delicate round of applause.

"That's why it's named Stinger" I pointed out. "Sometimes it buzzes even before it's thrown."

"It's a fine weapon Odin." Loki replied. "Do you mind if I try?"

I eagerly agreed, desiring has approval and Loki went to withdraw the knife from the tree trunk. He backed up to where I still stood and threw the knife awkwardly, appearing to have never before thrown a knife, or anything for that matter.

The knife couldn't have been said to have flown at all. It flopped and spun and sounded like a wasp spiraling out of the sky, rather than one zooming through the air. Landing with a thud a few feet away, it lay awaiting me to retrieve it.[13]

I couldn't help but laugh at his effort, I bad habit I had picked up from the giants of the plain, I suppose.

"You appear to need to a lot of practice yourself", I said. "I've seen some Vanir girls who can throw better than that."

Loki wasn't laughing with me. His upper lip curled into a snarl just long enough for me to notice, before morphing into a forced-looking smile.

"What's a Vanir, Odin? I know as much about your people as I do about throwing pretty trinkets."

My brows grew heavy and hung down over my eyes while I processed what Loki had said. To me, my knife was strong and powerful, not to be thought of in the terms he had used. I wasn't sure what he meant, so I gave him the benefit of the doubt, assuming the perceived insult was unintended.

"The Vanir are not my people. They are like us, but different in many ways; much like you and I seem to be so different from one another. They live out in the wilds and rule the kingdom of nature, so in a way, they rule the Ironwood too."

"One thing's for certain, the Vanir girls are fond of pretty trinkets and I believe on any day a Vanir goddess could throw one of their own better than you've done here. Let's try again. I'll show you how." I said, answering Loki's question, unable to withhold a barb of my own.

Loki's fake smile turned into a real one as far as I could tell, and he let out a short of a laugh.

"Okay Odin. I suppose I could use some instruction. Show me what to do."

I picked up Stinger and handed it back to him, giving him what I felt was the most basic of instruction before telling him to try again. At this, I backed away to a safe distance and waited to see now he would do.

Loki, moving smoothly, as if he'd been throwing things all his life, which, in hindsight, is probably close to the truth, cocked his arm and let Stinger fly. The knife began to buzz and sing as it left his hand and continued to do so as it narrowly missed the intended tree trunk. It seemed to fly straight and swift as it missed every tree thereafter, streaking through the forest. Had I been along for the ride I'd have realized the knife wasn't flying such a straight forward path at all. Although terrible luck was responsible for a large measure of what happened next, my intuition now tells me there was a bit of ill will guiding it[14] over the intervening years since then, I've learned that Loki's magic is always an equal mixture of what he wants and what he deserves.

The knife flew through the forest for quite a ways before finding a place to stop. One of the Ironwood's unique standing stones, graven with runes, stood resolute in Stinger's path and didn't flinch when the blade unsuccessfully attempted to impale it.

Although the knife buzzed wasp like as it flew, when it met the stone, it sounded more like wind escaping the tail-end of a mosquito. There, after unknown centuries of life, Stinger met its end at the hands of the mischief-maker, Loki. The blade shattered into several pieces and all that was left besides the shards was the smoothly wrought handle. The pieces fell to the forest floor in a meaningless array.

I could hardly see the distant stone through the crowded trees, but I immediately knew what had happened. I had built a friendship with my knife and it hurt my heart when it came to an end.

Loki offered an insultingly half-hearted apology. "Oops", but I had only to glance at him before he understood that this was no time for play.

I could feel the skin of my face flush with heat as I walked slowly to where lay the remains of my weapon. I knelt down and gazed at the damage, accounting for all of the broken blade.

Stinger had split into nine pieces, counting the handle.[15] Removing my hat, I methodically placed the shards in its crown before folding it up and fitting it into my bag.

By now, Loki was at my shoulder.

"Sorry for breaking your knife", he said, though he didn't really sound remorseful. "Maybe we can find you another one."

I looked up at Loki before standing to face him. He backed away when he saw the grave expression I wore.

"Stinger was not just any knife. No other knife could replace it. This is something you may not be able to understand, but I appreciate your apology nonetheless. All things must come to an end, but if I will it, this end will only be a new beginning."

"I will have the pieces forged into something new, though I don't yet know what. Let's go wherever it is you're leading me now. I'm ready to clean up."

Wunjo

We walked back toward the path we'd been on and resumed our journey quietly. Loki could probably tell I was in no mood to talk. As we moved on, I began thinking and reflecting as I tended to do at times like this.

"What can I learn from this?" I asked myself silently. "Is it my fault Stinger is broken, or should I be angry with Loki?"

To the first question, I had to devote more thought, but to the second, I understood then, that placing blame was a complicated task.

"Stinger is broken, and nothing can be done to take it back, least of all, being angry."

Although at the time, I had paid it little heed, but the rune that had been carved into the stone my knife had stuck was imprinted on my memory. It had been high up on the rock face, barely visible but it had called but to me, its magic reaching out and sending images into my consciousness.

As I knelt in the soil at its base, gazing at the pieces of my knife, I felt the yellow sky of a hail storm hanging above me. I heard the ripping leaves as the ice fell through the tree canopy. Though my mind's eye, I saw the icy mist rising from the ground as thousands of hailstones dotting the forest floor began to melt in the warmth of the day. I didn't know what to make if this daydream, but I took it as a good omen, even though thinking of it that way seemed strange to me at the time.[2]

As we walked I decided to strike up a conversation to break the oppressive silence.

"Loki? Do you have many friends out here?"

Loki furrowed his brow for a moment before answering.

"There are other giants in these parts, but they are quick to anger and, apparently, can't take a joke. Any friendships I make never last long. Most of the others seem to take themselves too seriously. I guess that's why I like you so much. You've got thick skin."

"That probably came from my dad's side" I said. "I like you too, even though you're a giant and you do things like one. I have to admit, I'm pretty upset about you breaking my knife, but I realize that breaking things is in your nature, so I should have seen it coming."

Loki knitted his brow again, while he obviously struggled to interpret this bit of insight.

"Things break" he finally said. "I didn't do it on purpose." A blatant lie.

I knew he hadn't liked the way I had picked on him, but was unable to admit it himself. I allowed him this.

"I'm sorry I broke it though. I know it meant a lot to you."

"Things break Loki. You're right about that. Some good will come of it though, as long as we choose for that to be so. Bad would come of it if that's what we chose, but I choose the good, so, well may it be."[3]

Struck by my ideals, I looked ahead through the treetops and caught a glimpse of the sun's swirling light and it made me glad to be on the path Loki and I walked.

"Do you have many friends back on the plain Odin?'

I answered absentmindedly, "No", before snapping from my reverie.

"There are my brothers and the giants. I agree with you about the giants. They are difficult to get along with, but you seem to be different. Maybe my expectations are what's wrong with them. Maybe I want them to be too much like me. My brothers are a lot like me, I now see, but even so, we aren't the best of friends. We don't' dislike each other, of course, but there is a distance because we are drawn toward our own interests. One of my brothers always has to have his own way and the other is too dreamy, always with his head in the clouds. I guess, honestly, I'm a mixture of both[4] other than that, the Vanir only show up at certain times of the year and we don't easily mix company."

I fixed on a round rock and kicked it down the path we walked.

"Now that I think about it, maybe the reason I don't have many friends is because I do the very same unlikeable things I hold against everybody else."

I found the presence of mind to look up from one last kick to the rock.

Loki looked at me and smiled, then laughed out loud.

"God, I know you're sad about your knife and all, but lighten up a little."

He quickly changed the subject. "The river's up ahead! I'll race you." Loki took off running before I could process what was happening. It didn't take long for me to catch up though, and only for a moment was Loki able to keep pace with me. I easily passed him and got far ahead. I never stopped until I reached the river bank. Turning around to see where my travel mate was, I discovered him nowhere in sight. The short path from the woods to the water was empty, tall grass bordering it on each side. I removed my satchel and lay it beside my staff in the shorter grass by the water front. Removing my drinking horn from the bag, I filled it from the cool water and drank deeply while I waited.

A moment later Loki came casually strolling down the wooded path, whistling a tune.

"What happened Loki?" I yelled at him playfully. "I thought you wanted to race?"

Loki smiled, breaking his whistle.

"We raced until you beat me; I don't know why you ran all the way here.[5]

I'm sure my confusion at this line of reasoning was able to be read upon my face, but Loki skillfully ignored it saying, "Why aren't you bathing yet, or do you not know how?"

I couldn't help but enjoy his deliberate ignorance.

"Oh, I know how," I said as I began removing my boots. "I've got some laundry to do as well, so don't mistake what comes next us, how did you put it, the custom of the plain."

I jumped up to my bare feet and ran fully clothed toward the water, doing a cannonball on the way in. After a moment below the surface, I came up a few yards downstream.

"Hey, Loki! You wanna try your luck at another race? I bet I can beat you swimming upstream to that sandy place."

I held my arm above the surface long enough to point to a small beach a good distance away.

"What'll you bet me?" Loki said in a flat tone, as if we were now negotiating a business deal.[6]

Apparently gambling was something he actually took seriously.

I hadn't meant to bet anything, but now that Loki and called me on it, I felt the need to go along. I was sure I would beat him in this competition as easily as I had in the foot race. All I had to do, I surmised, was get ahead by a little and he would give up. That meant I could spend all of my energy in the first part of the race, then take my time the rest of the way.

After forming my strategy I placed my bet.

"I'll wager my knife. It's all I've got of any worth. What will you put up?"

Loki looked at me like I was a fool.[7]

"What do I want with your broken knife? Do you think I'm that easy to trick?"

"Take it or leave it" I told him. "Now what'll you bet?'

"I'll tell you a secret my mother told me about my future."[8]

"And why would I care about your future?" I asked. If I'd known then what I know now, I might have swam harder.

"You'll just have to win to find out, won't you?"

I wasn't afraid for a moment that I'd lose, but I wasn't racing him to win what he bet. I was simply racing for the thrill of victory, something that's clouded my vision from time to time since then.[9]

"To even the odds I'll keep all but my shoes on as well." Loki said before pulling off his dusty leather slippers while he still stood. Once barefoot, he ran and dived into the water without the slightest splash.

I should have taken that as a sign.

For a moment, we swam side by side, fighting the current to stay abreast.

"Are you ready?" he asked me.

"Ay" was all I replied.

"I'll start with you" said Loki, giving me the advantage.

My heart beat faster, as it always does at the thought of completion. A smile stretched across my face in anticipation of my coming victory. I readied myself and counted to three out loud.

"One...Two...Three!" and in a torrent of motion we began swimming toward our goal.

Although I could not see with my face buried in the churning water that my thrashing arms was creating, Loki later explained to me how he won the race.

He ducked his head under water and after a short time the surface where he swam must have budged upward, so he said, a wave anticipating his return to the surface. He was probably exaggerating, knowing Loki.

He claimed to have completely left the water as he burst from the depths, splashing his widening side into the water below him.

The rest I can imaging based on what I saw for myself.

He swam with his arms straight against his body and his legs moving together as one. He darted through the water like a fish, changing as he swam. His clothes took on a silvery shimmer. His face might have been mistaken as being red from exertion, but that idea would have evaporated when it changed into the red face of a salmon.

When I asked him how long he had to practice to move his legs in unison, he told me he didn't have to because, once he was in the form of a fish, he no longer had any legs to worry over. They were replaced by a powerful fin, and in this case, it was driving him upstream so fast I barely managed to glimpse him as he passed me, and even then, I didn't realize it was him.

I swam powerfully, as I usually do, and after some distance, as planned, I slowed my pace. That's about the time the giant salmon swam past me. I had the wherewithal…to glance behind me and I didn't see my opponent anywhere.

"Must've given up already." I thought, but by the time I was approaching the beach, Loki was already there and was changing back into a boy.

I came out of the water, standing waist deep, in time to see the final stages of the transformation. Watching in wonder, I saw his arms grow out of what were once short side-fins. His clothes appeared scaly before returning to their original texture. His protruding, fishy under bite became a beguiling smile and his set of foggy, dead-looking fish eyes were once again bright and knowing. He stood, defiantly watching my approach.

"So, a small fire isn't the only thing you can change into? Now I feel like I'm the one who's been tricked." I said accusingly.

"We haven't known each other for very long, Odin; I'm sure I still have much to learn about you as well."

I couldn't help but frown; not because of Loki's trick, but because I was thinking of what I had lost in this bet. I shouldn't have ever risked losing something of so much worth to me.[10]

"That, you do" is all I could manage to say.

"I suppose you'll want your winnings now" I was saying when both of us were distracted by the unexpected, high howl of a wolf cub.

We turned to look at the same time and saw, not only one, but a pair of starved-looking pups standing at the edge of the water, fearlessly staring us down.

They snarled and snowed their small, needlelike teeth. Their steely gray fur stood on end everywhere, not helping to disguise their skinny, bony frames. The wolves both had their heads down low against the ground, looking at Loki and

I along the rippling, wrinkled ridges of their snouts.

Apparently these young wolves believed they had found themselves a meal, though what would be lunch was ten times their size. It was clear these pups had hugs appetites.

"It appears as if they've left their pack before coming of age" I observed as I slunk down low, needlessly trying to make myself appear smaller.

"I bet they're starved."

"The odds are in your favor Odin," Loki looked at me mischievously, "but I'm game. What would you bet?"

"I didn't mean it like that. I'm just saying it looks like they're hungry. I guess I've got to choose my words carefully around you."

"I've got some meat in my bag. Stay here and I'll swim back down and get it."

"Oh yes, it's clear we've got no choice but to feed these stays." he said in sarcastic protest.

Even unwillingly, Loki did as he was asked, but as soon as I was gone he must have changed back into a fish to tease the poor creatures.

He told me he was poking his fish face out of the water, but they dared not enter. "Not very courageous pests" was how he put it.[11]

Only a few minutes had passed before I crept back up the river bank carrying everything we'd left behind. My satchel now bulged with all it had once held, along with both of our shoes.

I sat down near the water's edge and began unloading, removing the shoes, then my drinking horn, my folded hat and broken knife, then finally the hunk of salted meat I had wrapped in cloth.

"If I had a knife," I said to the huge salmon swimming nearby, "I'd cut it up for all to share, but as things stand, I'll have to give them the whole thing."[12]

After unwrapping it, I tossed the meat in the direction of the wolves while I chided Loki.

"Stop picking on them and come out of the water already. I'm half-inclined to eat you if you remain a fish for much longer, especially now that I'm giving my lunch away to these mutts."

Loki quickly changed form, probably only to get the last word in, before he sat down to watch the ensuing battle.

"I would have just as soon eaten them instead of feeding them, so don't try to hold that over my head."

The wolf cubs had my attention as they descended upon this easier pray. At first, they only sniffed at the large cut of meat, but it wasn't long at all before one of them pounced and began gnawing at it.

The other Wolfling took this as the signal to do the same and afterward, they never managed to share their meal peacefully; as soon as one of them would relent in this biting and tugging, the other would try to make off with the whole thing. Neither one would get very far before his sibling took notice and latched back onto their shared meal.

While the wolves ate, I took up my horn. After dipping it in the water I held it up in the air, saying "Here's to friends who fare forth freely."

I took a long pull from it, spilling water from the horn's sides down my face and chest.

I handed the horn to Loki and told him to take a drink.

He received it with a smile and held it up as I had done, obviously finding this little custom funny.

"To me, here, the fourth fair friend." he said, taking his own, less messy drink.

I looked at him crosswise.

"What's that supposed to mean?" I asked.

"There are four of us now" he said "and I am, by far, the best looking of the bunch. I think I deserve some recognition."

I just shook my head.

"We can't yet say these wolves are our friends and I'm pretty sure I'm the better looking between the two of us."

Loki laughed at that, as if I'd been joking, then continued on in a serious tone.

"One minute you want to feed them and the next you aren't sure whether they are your friends. Which is it? can't you give your friendship to anyone ungrudgingly? It seems like you think you'll run out if you share it with too many.[13]

I felt my face go slack. He had spoken the truth. Loki was good at that, but most of the time he only spoke the truth when it would sting.

Loki pointed toward the wolves, who were still competing for the fast-shrinking cut of boar's meat.

"They're hungry little beasts, aren't they?"

In my desire to avoid Loki's revelation, I was able to quickly change my mood.

"Yes" I said with a chuckle, "neither of them is very generous. They'd each have the whole thing if they could, and not one of them could possibly eat it all."

"Greed and gluttony." Loki said.

I looked at him curiously.

"What do you mean by that?" I asked.

Loki thought for a moment before responding.

"Greed is when you want more of something just for the sake of having it and gluttony is when you eat more of something just for the sake of eating it. These are things we giants do know something about."

I nodded in understanding.

"On the plain we have different words for them. We call one Geri and the other Freki, but they mean the same thing as what you said."

"These cubs need names and if I have a say in it, that's what they'd be called. "See the one who keeps trying to eat as much as he can before his brother does?"

Loki pointed at the offender. "That one?"

"Yap." I said. "He'll be Freki, and the one who keeps trying to steal away with the whole thing will be Geri."

"So, you've named them now" Loki said. "You know, once you've given someone a name, you've got to give them a gift to go along with it, right?"[14]

"Yeah, I know. How do you know? That's the real question. "That's the same thing we do at home."

"Well, that's the way it's done here too. So what'll it be?"

"I'd say I've already given them a gift; look at now fat they are now. They can hardly stand up with their swollen bellies."

The newly named wolflings, Geri and Freki, lay, lazily licking their chops, no longer so interested in devouring us.

"That doesn't count my friend. Loki pointed out. "You'd already given them the meat before you gave them names."

"Well, I don't have anything else in my satchel worth giving them. I'd give them my boots to gnaw on, but we've still got a journey ahead of us."

At that, I began putting my boots back on while I spoke.

"I'll need them a while longer I think."

Loki followed suit, slipping into his worn leather shoes.

"You've given me the gift of friendship haven't you?" he said. "Have you run out of that as well?"

"No" I said, "I don't suppose I have."

Looking at the pups, I rhetorically spoke.

"Will you be my friends, Geri and Freki?"

I assumed they didn't understand me.

They both looked at me though, either snarling or smiling – it was hard to tell – and howled a pair of long, wolfy howls just to make sure I understood the message.

"Well then," I said as I began to repack my scattered belongings, "I guess there are four of us after all."

46

I reached down to pet the newly named Freki, but as my hand got closer his lip raised, exposing his threatening little teeth.

"Slow to warm up huh?" I said to the wolf cub. "I guess we'll have to work on this friendship thing a bit."

Loki must have found this spectacle amusing, because he giggled like a maiden before offering his opinion, unsolicited.

"Yep, four faithful friends we are. Lovely Loki, two wary wolves and Odiferous Odin."

"I've bathed" I reminded Loki.

He laughed.

"I'm afraid that didn't do the trick, unless you just always smell this way."

"Maybe you're just smelling your upper lip for all of the filth that spills below it."

I trailed off as I picked up my folded hat which still contained Stinger.

I opened it, exposing its contents, gazing within sadly for a moment.

"I suppose you'll want this" I said, extending the hat towards Loki.

He didn't move to take it from me, but spoke "Not now; why don't you hold onto it for me. I don't have any pockets and it would be difficult for me to keep up with it."

I get the hat down and thought for a second.

"It's yours. Don't' forget, but I'll do as you ask."

I looked from my upturned hat to the wadded piece of cloth which the boar's meat had been wrapped in. Straightening it out, I transferred Stinger's remains into it then used my share to secure the bundle.

After placing it back in my bag and pulling my hat down over my ears I stood with my staff.

"If we're going to make it to the distant edge of the forest before Sunna descends we'll need to get moving. Come on friends, we've got a journey to make."

Loki stood, dusted off his pants and straightened his shirt while mumbling to himself."

"You'll see how very distant that is sooner than you'd expect."

I looked at him, pretending I hadn't heard.

"What was that Loki?"

"Oh, nothing" he said. "Let's get this over with. There's plenty of fun to be had before the day's end, and seeing the edge of the forest will be the least of it."

"Which path should be take, Loki?" I asked, containing my curiosity at his allusion.

Loki walked past me, dismissively saying "Just follow the river. It flows right over the edge you seem to be so eager to discover."

I caught in at Loki's heels along the narrow game path next to the river, the wolves in line behind us, following at a distance.

"That's an odd way of phrasing it. Wouldn't the river flow past the edge, and not over it? What's beyond the edge of the forest anyway?"

I was an excitable lad, prone to excessive questions for which I really needed no answers.

"Why don't you just describe it to me?" "I said, reaching the end of my litany.

As he walked, Loki looked back over his shoulder for a moment and said "Let me just say, so I don't spoil your surprise, that this is giant territory and the deeper into the ironwood we go, the bigger and older the giants get."[15]

"Okay," I said, ignoring his subtext, "but what's that got to do with the lay of the land beyond the forest?"

"You'll see." Loki replied, and I sensed he was done talking about it.

We journeyed for some time, along grassy paths and rocky ones, and when we came to an especially difficult stretch of riverbank, with large boulders and what appeared to be huge standing stones lain on their sides, Loki and I began having trouble easily navigating the obstacles.

The wolves, too, were having trouble, but they still remained elusive, hanging back some distance from us until we had to scale an embankment too high for them to negotiate.

Although Loki and I were aware of our wild friends following us, we allowed them their distance until they decided for themselves to come closer. They had managed to keep up thus far, but this obstacle proved to be the decision maker for them. They could either subject themselves to contact with us, or part ways.

Atop the large stone Loki and I looked back at them.

"What do you suppose we should do?" I asked Loki.

"I don't really care." he said "Let's leave them behind."

I was reluctant, we'd only just pledged our friendship to them, but if they'd not allow me to touch them, I had little choice.

When we turned to dismount the other side of the stone, the pups scrambled at the opposite side, whining and howling, trying to find a way up.

"So, hungry ones," I asked as I knelt over them, "will you allow me to assist you?"

They continued their pleas.

"If you bite me, I'll toss you into the river and be on my way" I said as I reached down toward them.

They didn't resist.

I took up Geri by the scruff of his neck, then Freki, and carried them, curled up like two sacks of flour over the obstacle.[16]

Elhaz

The sounds of the flowing water seemed to increase as we went. The water flowed faster as other creeks and small rivers joined with this one. The banks on either side of the waterway seemed to get further and apart, until the distance became too far to easily ford.

The path changed from rocks, to grass, to marshy wetland and back to rocks again. The sounds of the river continued to increase until they were too loud to equal what the fast-flowing river should have been making.

I couldn't help but take notice.

"Why's the river so loud Loki?" I had to shout to be heard.

"There's hardly any rapids, but it sounds like there's a giant roaring beneath the water."[2]

"We're near the edge Odin. I told you we wouldn't have far to go. That sound isn't the part of the river you see here. Some is the sound of the falls ahead. Just come on. We haven't got all day" he finally said impatiently "Let's get this over with."

The wolves and I followed Loki. The trees of the forest had grown massive and enormously thick this deep into the Ironwood, but I hadn't been paying attention to the way the trees suddenly stopped in the distance because of my preoccupation with the violence and noise of the river.

"If this is the edge of the forest" I observed to myself, "my world is not quite the place I imagine it was."

I had spent long hours picturing this journey and its end. In my mind, I would have traveled long and hard to arrive here, where I would have seen the forest gradually grow thinner, until it became another grassland, like Ida Plain. I had imagined mountains, or an ocean on the other side, but never this.[3]

The forest appeared as if it had been whole at one time and was torn apart. The large trees went right up to edge of a rocky cliff, some hanging over the side, barely clinging to the sheer rock face. The river flew into the void, where the other missing trees must have fallen, and roared so loud it threatened to drown out all thought in my mind.

Where I had pictured mountains or waves, there was nothing but a vast, mist-filled canyon with no perceptible end. The mist swirled and eddied where the river plunged in. There were cloudy tendrils in the distance and from within the mist, whale-like humps would surface, the size of islands, then descend again.

"Loki, Loki!" I exclaimed, pointing toward this sight. "There's something in there. What could it be?"

Loki, frowning uncharacteristically, replied, "That, kinsman, is our distant ancestor, Ymir. What you saw was only an elbow, a knee, or some other small body part. He thrashes in the mist, doing all in this power to keep the worlds within his grip."

"Worlds?" I said dreamily.[4]

"Do you hear the roar Odin?" He looked at me gravely. "That is not only the sound to the great river falling into the void…" The river spanning a mile or more poured endlessly into the unknown depths. "Ymir is roaring as well. All of the things you despise about the giants came from him, but as you have learned, there's some good, even in that. Without him, you and I wouldn't be here to hate him so."

I glared into the distance in thought. Geri and Freki sniffed at the edge and growled, probably thinking about devouring the old giant.

After a long silence, I spoke.

"There might still be some use for him after all. As things stand, Ymir serves no true and good purpose. He's strangling us all. I see his wyrd though, and I promise you this, his future is in my hands. Is there a way down there Loki?"

"Aah Ha!" Loki laughed loudly. "What do you intend to do, Odin Borson? Are you and your puppies going to tickle the great roarer? That's all you could manage with no weapons. He wouldn't even know you were there."

At first, I wanted to throttle Loki for his insolence, but then I considered what he was saying.

"You're right. I'll have to form a plan."

Loki stretched his arms out wide as his jaw hung open in exasperation, not having expected me to interpret his criticism in such a way.

I continued.

"Preparations must be made for such a task, out hear me; I shall return, and when I do, Ymir will be slain."[5]

Loki could probably tell this was the truth of the matter by how earnestly I spoke. Apparently not enjoying the thought of such serious business, he tried to distract me from my intensity.

"Hey, look at the sun. The day is wasting. We'll not have any more fun hanging around here, or trekking through the forest in the dark. The creatures that come out at night aren't what I'd call friendly. Come to think of it, I know a monster you could subdue, since you seem to be in the mood, who makes trouble for all who live in the Ironwood after the sun has set. If we go now we can catch him sleeping."

I must admit, I was intrigued.

"What sort of beast is this you speak of Loki?"

"It's, uh…"

Loki looked into the sky appearing mesmerized by something. I followed his gaze. There was nothing there but the clear blue of the evening sky, Sunna nearly halfway back down from her zenith, towards the Eastern horizon.

"It's a dragon!" he said excitedly.

"It's big and scaly and it breathes fire" the words seemed to tumble from his mouth as he smiled and nodded.

"It's guarding an ancient hoard of gold, stolen from the dwarves who used to live in his lair."

I was skeptical.

"What was with all the hesitation, Loki? You seem unsure."

"What? No!" he responded defensively. "I was just thinking about now frightful the beast is. He's such a pest. Always burning things, and, and oh, he stinks too, really bad, not that I've got anything against people who stink, Odin, no offense. But anyway, this dragon's a real meany."

"I'd be glad to help you," I said, "but as you've pointed out, we have no weapons. Unless you think tickling this one will actually work, we'll have to try again some other time."

"I've got an idea." Loki got even more excited than he already was. "I can show you a trick my father taught me that might help us in the weapons department."

"Now you've got my attention; I'm always game to learn a trick or two."

"Then a game it is" he gladly replied before he unexpectedly darted back into the forest as quick as a deer.

The wolves and I watched him for a second before we thought to follow, and even then, keeping up proved difficult.

He was shape-shifting as he ran, which made the effort all the more difficult. One moment he would bound over a fallen tree as a white-tailed deer, then he would scurry under a low-slung bough as a cotton-tailed rabbit. He changed from human form to that of a squirrel in two shakes of a wolf cub's tail.

Geri and Freki didn't seem to be having any trouble at all though. They both ran with their noses to the ground, moving confidently forward as they followed Loki's trail.

Now, I had to rely on them to direct me, as I frequently lost sight of our tricky companion. We were all making much quicker progress back into the than had been made on the trip to the Yawning Void.[6]

With the sun going down, her light managed to pierce the forest through its crowded tree trunks, casting long shadows where there began to appear the glowing eyes of creatures awaiting full darkness.

Loki didn't seem daunted by any of these creatures. Where he ran, they scattered. But I, ever wary, carried my staff across my chest with both hands, prepared to defend myself should any of them grow bold enough to attack. My courage was a stronghold. I would not allow my fear to rob me of clarity, or the will to press on.

Our group, now running in a zigzagging line, moved swiftly through the Ironwood toward a goal only Loki knew.

"Even more rocks now" I thought to myself. "Soon there will be nothing else" and I was not mistaken.

We seemed to be continuously running uphill, on an ever-tightening switch back.

"These stones; there's something about them."

I kept seeing the same symbol engraved upon them randomly as we went.

"It keeps pressing upon my mind. What is it? White fire. Flashing; no, exploding in the sky."[7]

The grass and the undergrowth of the forest was soon replaced by a ground covering of loose shale, slipping under foot, making the journey harder and slower.

Loki couldn't' keep up his fast pace under these conditions, even as he changed into the form of a mountain goat.

As I drew closer to him I yelled "That's more like you than any! Have you assumed your true form to introduce me to your father?"

"Blaah-eh-eh-eh" Loki bleated before returning to his red-heeded human form. "I mean, we're not going to meet my father. He only shows up when there's a storm brewing and then, not for very long. He's the opposite of what you'd call a fair weather friend, I suppose.'

"Don't get along very well then?" I asked.

"No, it's not that. We giants just aren't as tight knit as you gods I guess. Even though he's not around much, he's still my father and I've inherited enough from him to be grateful."[8]

"We're almost there now, so you can stop with the thousand questions. See that black outcropping up ahead? That's what I wanted to show you."

I looked up the now steep slope toward what Loki was pointing at. A large dark boulder appeared to be split down the middle like a cracked egg. The remains of the stone that had been together at one time lie scattered around it in glassy shards.

As we approached, Loki pointed at the crack in the stone.

"My father did this. He struck it once and the stone shattered. I wasn't here when it happened, but I saw him from a distance and when I came to look, I discovered the way this rock behaves."

"It's got a personality, you know. Some rocks just lie around. They're kind of lazy, but they're still good for something. You can stack them up and they'll stay put. Other rocks like to toll. They'll look for any way to keep going. A rolling rock will find its way down a mountainside and then, when it can't roll downhill anymore, it will find its way into a river and keep on rolling."[9]

"Oh yeah?" I said with a smile. "What sort of rock are you?"

Loki didn't respond and continued his speech.

"As I was saying, rocks have a sort of spirit about them and if you can talk to them and get to know them, you can find their purpose. This rock is a warrior, came to find out. Of course, it lost its battle with my father, but that just exposed its spirit to me."

"See this?"

Loki picked up a hefty piece of the black, glassy rock in one hand and a piece of hard shale in the other.

"There's something inside waiting to be revealed, something to make war with."

Loki struck the black obsidian with the shale and a portion of it flaked off.

"You've got to talk to the stone and it will tell you want it holds. I mean, you've got to talk to it with your imagination. Look at it and try to see what it's saying."

Loki struck it again and another large portion of glass flaked off and fell to the ground. He struck it again and again, and before long, it had begun to take shape.

At first, just a rough wedge with blunt edges, but soon, those began to sharpen into blades of serrated glass. The stone became and axe-head, and then a dagger.

Loki held it up for me to see once he had finished.

"See? I knew this was inside the stone when I picked it up. I gave it the gift of my energy and it gave me this gift in return. A gift for a gift. That's the law of the world, isn't it?" he looked at me, amused.

"Yes, it is, Loki. I wouldn't have expected your kind to understand such a thing. The Asa-folk abide by this law above all else. How do you know it?"

"Ha!" Loki scoffed. "You gods believe you came up with everything, don't you? The power of the gift is greater than any race or tribe. It's one of those universal things that's just a part of how the world works. The gift is as much a part of this rock as it is a part of you or I."[10]

I looked at the sky, then the ground and then, the back of my hand feeling like I'd been missing something all along.

"I'm sorry Loki, I still have much to learn." I said humbly."[11]

"As do I, my friend," Loki said. "Now what do you think of this fine weapon? It's no Stinger, but I think it worthy of slaying a stinking dragon any day."

"It's a fine weapon and good for many things, I'm sure, but I've been told tales of dragons all my life and none have been so daring as to get close enough to battle a dragon with a knife."

An idea came upon me in a flash of inspiration.

"I've got it!"[12]

I threw down my satchel and immediately began digging to the bottom of it.

"It's got to be here somewhere. I was going to trap some game if I had to, but that's not likely anymore."

I removed the bundle containing Stinger's remains.

"Here it is!" I said as I loosened the cat-gut I'd tied it with.

I carefully replaced the bundle inside my bag.

"Let me see the weapon Loki." I held out my hand to receive it.

Loki held out his own, empty hand, the dagger still gripped in the other.

"Here it is Odin. Can't you see it?" He waved the dagger away from me.

I wasn't sure what he was up to.

"Yes, I can indeed see it, but why are you giving me your empty hand and not what I've asked for?'

"Oh?" Loki said, "I thought this was some kind of Aesir greeting or something. I was wondering the same when you did it."

"I'm holding out my hand so you will put the cursed piece of stone in it. Does everything have to be a game with you? Sometimes you're as sharp as this blade and others you're as dull as your rolling stone."

Loki, looking satisfied with himself, finally passed the stone dagger to me.

"You learn and I play." he said. "That's our nature. In fact, I think I learn when I play. Every time I anger you, I learn more about you. What does all of that anger teach you? Does it teach you about me?

"Another trick" I thought to myself, but then reconsidered and seriously weighed the answer.

"No," I told him as I turned the faceted stone over in my hand, "I have only learned about myself along with you, I suppose. A gift for a gift, right?"

This creature, this giant, was full of surprises.

I picked up my staff without further discussion, then, after tucking the dagger in my belt, I found a sharp, sturdy piece of glass at my feet. Cutting deeply into the end of my staff, I wedged the stone into the wood. I used yet another blunt stone to hammer this wedge further into the wood until it was sufficiently split for my purposes.

I removed the wedge, replaced it with the dagger and secured it all with the share, holding it out in admiration.

"I think this will do, don't you?"

I looked to Loki for affirmation.

"Indeed, it's a mighty weapon now," the trickster replied. The fiery serpent won't stand a chance."

"I think you're right about that my friend" I said while thrusting the newly made spear at the air before me. "Now where is his lair? The day is drawing to a close."

"It's on the other side of this very mountain. Up toward the summit there's a cava that's always spewing smoke and ash. I've seen it from a long way off and even at that distance, the sooty, blackened rock at the cave's mouth is obvious. It's pretty frightening Odin. We don't have to go if you're scared."

I couldn't help but smile at Loki's jokes by now. He knew I was looking forward to the coming battle.

"What are we waiting for?" I said, "Come on wolflings, there's war to make!"

The pups howled their assent.

"Let's go then," Loki said, wearing his own grin, and we all followed him once more as he began the trek, around the treacherous mountainside.

Hagalaz

The shale made for difficult travel, and there was no discernable path, but our group found the way steadily around the mountain top. The forest below could be seen from this vantage, and in the distance, Ida Plain.

As our war-band trekked, I looked Westward toward home in the dwindling light. The wide plain was beautiful to behold and reminded me of my family and tribe. I thought fondly of working with them and eating with my brothers around a warm hearth fire. It finally occurred to me that even though my brothers and I ware different, we had one very important thing in common; we were family. In light of that fact, our differences were small by comparison.[2]

I took note that I hadn't eaten all day, but for some reason I was not at all hungry. Ever since meeting Geri and Freki, the thought of food no longer plagued me. I was thirsty, for sure, but for something, at that time, I couldn't quite put my finger on. I wouldn't learn what that something was until some time later, but that's another story.[3]

I realized then that I was ready to begin my journey home. This last thing had to be done though, because I had committed myself to it already, but after it was complete, I told myself, I would be on my way. The time for Loki's fun and games was drawing to a close.

"Tell me, Loki, what's this dragon done lately to warrant us killing him?"

I broke the silence.

Loki thought for a moment.

"Uh, I already told you. He's got a bunch of stolen dwarf gold."

"No, no, Loki. What's new? You said that happened long ago. What's he done lately?"

"Well, he sits in a cave and breathes fire. I'd say that's pretty threatening. What if he came and destroyed everything?"

"Has he come out?"

"No, but he could." Loki said defensively. "Isn't that enough?"

"Well," I said thoughtfully, "It seems like most of this creature's power lies in your fear, rather than in his might.[4]

Loki shook his head vigorously and in the process tripped over a rock.

"Stupid rock..." he mumbled under his breath as he caught his balance.

"Trying to talk yourself out of this one? What's that smell Odin? Did you miss a spot when you bathed, or did you just make a new mess in your pants?"

"No, I'm no coward, but I'll not be fooled into a wrongful act just because you like to destroy things for the fun of it. I need to know that this beast has actually done something wrong before we just barge in there and kill him for no good reason."

"Oh," Loki said, as if he had suddenly understood, "wall in that case, he was walking in the forest one day when he farted such a monstrous, fiery fart, that many woodland fairies and sprites tragically lost their lives where they stood. Is that not offensive enough?"

I looked at my friend, smiling ruefully. I'm still fond of fart jokes to this day.

"I think we'll have to wait and see what the situation is like when we get there, before any dragon-slaying happens."

Loki shrugged.

"Whatever you say buddy. It's a dragon; you've got a spear; we're on our way."

We didn't have much further to go. Up ahead, the mouth of a large cave gaped open and rolling, black smoke poured from its roof, leaving only enough space below to walk upright without being smothered.

The wolves sat beside us as we stood before the cave, contemplating what our next move should be.

Nothing was visible within the cave but a faint orange glow, which appeared like a small ember burning beneath a mound of ash.

"What do you suppose that light is, Loki?"

Loki shook his head slowly and shrugged.

"I couldn't say. Maybe the dragon is yawning and that's the fire in his belly. Maybe he's sleeping with one eye open. Could be a mound of shining gold, but I guess there's only one way to know for sure, although, now that we're here, I'm having some second thoughts of my own. I don't think this is such a good idea."

"Now, now Loki. You've bean goading me this whole time. I'm not gonna let you cry off when we've come this far. If nothing else, we'll go see if the beast poses any threat. If it attacks, then we'll be left no choice but to fight, but if it's nothing but a friendly worm with bad breath, we'll know that leaving him in peace is the right thing to do."

"It's time we did what we came for, Loki. This was your idea, so by all rights, you should have the honor of going first. I wouldn't want to steal your glory."

Loki patted me on the back with a laugh. "No, my friend, by all means. You can win the day. There'll be songs written about you someday. Go ahead. I'll be right behind you."

Of course, I didn't hesitate. I knew the value of Loki's gift and accepted it graciously, walking into the darkness with Geri and Freki by my side.

The floor of the cave was barely visible in the poor light, but what could be seen appeared to be molten black stone, bubbling up from the fire that lived within the mountain. At first, I was afraid to step where the large bubbles had formed, worried I might sink into whatever lay beneath, but after testing with my toe, I realized the ground was firm, and the bubbles, which once must have been fluid, were now hard as rocks, frozen in time before bursting.

"It looks as if the entire floor is cobbled with stone bubbles," I said to Loki.

Some were large domes of blue and black glass, seeming about to burst, others were small, like a thousand black eyes staring from the floor. I made my way carefully, concentrating on every step while forming a strategy for now we might confront an angry dragon.

The wolves and I were so fixated on what lay ahead, we didn't notice what was behind us. Had we been better aware, we'd have noticed nobody there. Loki had either disappeared, or tucked his dangling tail and run. It wouldn't have made any difference to me though. Loki's presence wasn't required to reinforce my courage. I had made up my mind to face whatever was within, and sparing no other choices, I would not be turning back.

My satchel lay heavy against my thigh. I paused

for a moment, adjusting it to the rear so it wouldn't get in the way, then I pulled my cap down tight upon my head. Satisfied, I gripped my spear out before me, pointing the way deeper into the darkness.

All of my attention was on the orange glow up ahead, which had not changed since entering the cave; had not changed, that is, until it simply vanished with a wink. The wolf cubs stopped in unison, growling deep and low. The dragon had closed its eye.

"Loki?" I whispered to nobody. "Our foe stirs. Be on your guard."

I stepped softly once, my foot narrowly missing a fragile glass bubble. I stepped once more and was not so lucky. When my toe pressed down, the glass shattered and fall with such a clatter, I suspected my brothers back on the plain might have heard it.

"Yieeep!" the wolves yelped in fear.

Obviously the creature had heard it too, because not just one glowing ember reappeared, but two; a pair of angry eyes, then a third; a large, glowing, toothy smile, then two more lights flared like torches; nostrils, blowing molten fire.

The time to act had come. "Charge, Loki.

Attack!" I yelled, but Loki had already begun his attack by then.

The cluster of lights moved toward me with terrible speed. Geri and Freki shrank back then ran away entirely, yelping all the way. A roar reverberated through the cava, so fearsome, even the stone walls shivered.

I too was afraid, but it was impossible for me to run. I leaned forward, thrusting my spear out ahead of me and charged at the oncoming dragon, issuing a war-cry to rival the monster's. We ran at one another like clashing forces of nature, neither willing to bend to the other, leach, determined to carry this battle out until one, or both of us were destroyed.[6]

As the dragon ran, he blew out plumes of noxious smoke and explosions of searing flame, engulfing everything in his path, filling every inch of the cave he called home with swirling fire.

"Loki was right..." I thought to myself as I bore down on my enemy through the suffocating flames. This thought was unfinished before I kept into the smoke and fire, spear raised for the kill.

The fire laid waste to my clothes. The brim of my hat burned through, leaving nothing to shield my face. Though I didn't know, it when it happened, the strap of my satchel snapped and the bag fell to the floor of the cave.

The glassy tip of my spear went pointedly into the gaping mouth of the dragon, shortly before I too was consumed whole. I had leapt into what I thought would be my end and what I hoped would be this monster's.

As my spear entered the spewing fire of the dragon's jaws, the great serpent began to evaporate and shrink where it stood. I plunged forward with my spear thrusting at thin air and my lungs expelling the burned, sulfur-tasting air, I gave a cry of pure determination and passed into the darkness of what I thought was the dragon's throat.

I was met with great surprise though, when I rolled to a stop on the floor of the pitch black cave. Looking around, my eyes slow to adjust to the darkness after the blinding light of the dragon-fire, I saw movement behind me and the same dull, orange glow, deep within the mountain, as if it had never moved.

With my spear at the ready, I approached whatever was stirring in the shadows.

"Holy cow, Odin!" Loki yelled excitedly as he stood to greet me. "You almost killed me!"

I was confused at that.

"Almost killed you? What do you mean? That was you? You were the Dragon? You! You. Almost. Killed. Me!" I spoke as my rage boiled inside me.

Loki just laughed his uncontrolled, obnoxious laugh.

"You were supposed to run away. At least you're wolves knew what to do."

"Well," I said, suppressing my anger momentarily, "my wolves are only looking for an easy meal, while I am trying to protect my friends! I couldn't run! I had no choice!"

"You're a better man than I then. You were pretty scary though too. Heck, I almost ran away, and I was the dragon!"

"So, where's the real dragon Loki? Have you been lying this whole time?"

Loki looked like a scorned child.

"I wasn't lying-lying. I mean, obviously there's something bad in hare that has to do with fire. Look down there." Loki pointed toward the glowing depths of the cave. "Something burned this place up and I don't think it was just for the fun of it. Who's to say it wasn't a dragon?"

"Loki, I've had enough of your games for today.

What I ought to do is beat you senseless," I grabbed him by the neck of his shirt, "like one of your giant-kin would have done a long time ago." I was yelling now. "I was ready to go home a long time ago, long before you led me into this hole."

My rage was growing hot, but before it could explode, we were distracted by whatever had been sleeping deeper in the cave. Without a moment to react otherwise, I turned to face what came.[8]

The orange glow which had once bean dull, grew blindingly bright. The smoke which had once only flowed along the ceiling, now billowed forcefully. The air in the cave smelled of sulfur once again and rushed away, toward the opening in the mountainside.

Loki never had a chance to run, and run I'm certain he would have, had I not been standing in his way. The flaming heart of the mountain careened toward us faster than could be reckoned and once again, I was prepared for battle.

In the brightness and radiant heat of the onrushing flow of liquid fire, I could see the face of a screaming fire giant which made Loki's dragon look friendly by comparison.

I remember, as if in slow motion, tossing my spear up and catching it above my head. I braced myself, one foot in front of the other, and exerted every bit of godly force within me as I launched it at this real enemy.

The flowing magma churned and roiled as it rushed toward us. Loki shrank down upon his knees, screaming in fear and crying tears which steamed away in the heat of his coming destruction. I smiled and threw the spear over his head, toward the angry etin.[9]

It flew like a bolt of lightning, straight and true, covering the short distance between us in the space of one of Loki's fearful heartbeats and buried its glassy point in the giant's aye, ending its long, destructive life.

The magma immediately began to darken, but it did not slow its pace, leaving me no choice but to flee.

"Loki! Run!" I yelled, having quickly forgotten my anger, but Loki was beyond hearing me in his terror.

I grabbed him by the nape of the neck, like I had done Geri and Freki, and dragged him from danger along the floor of the darkening cave, all the way to the entrance.

Geri and Freki stood waiting outside, howling us a greeting as we came out of the cave.

We both collapsed; Loki from cowardice and I,

from exhaustion.

"Are you hurt Loki?" I asked as I lay, trying to catch my breath.

Loki didn't respond. Ha only lay on his back, head turned enough to see the remains of the fire giant spreading like molasses from the mouth of the cave.

"Not so much fun when you're the one being attacked, is it Loki? Look at you, not a single burn. I'd light you on fire myself if it weren't for how badly being dragged tore you up. It pleases me to see you in such bad shape."

Loki's head lulled toward me, the weak smile on his face, quickly replaced by a grimace of pain.

"You still stink, but I prefer sulfur and burnt hair to poop. How about you take a look at yourself? How'd you get so filthy?" he said, apparently forgetting he was the one who had charred me to a crisp, as well as the fact that I was just about to wring his neck.

"You seem to have misplaced your things." he continued. "You should try to be more responsible."

I looked at my shoulder, then felt for my bag, only then realizing it was gone.

"Stinger." I whispered, the loss of this treasure felt for the third time that day.

"My satchel must have fallen off in our retreat. We have to go Pack and look for it."

"What?" Loki said in surprise. "I'm not going back in there. I was stupid to risk it the first time and I'm especially not going to risk my life again for a broken knife."

"I don't care what you do," I said frustratedly, "but I'm going back, with, or without you."

Loki grunted and rolled onto iris stomach as I got to me feet. By the time I was walking back into the cave he yelled at me.

"Alright, god, I'm coming, but just make sure you don't get yourself into any more trouble. We've had more than our fair share of that today. Just find the knife and let's go."

Side by side, we carefully walked toward the hole, over the, now, solidified remains of the slain giant.

I noticed that the old glass bubbles and humps had been covered over and replaced by new ones. Where I had broken them, both in entering the cave and dragging Loki out, fresh and fragile domes of blue and black glass had frozen with other bubbles formed within them. However carefully we attempted to walk, crushing the delicate formations was unavoidable.

"Careful Odin, there might be more giants in here," Loki whispered.

"I'm almost positive there are, though I don't see any sign of them now.

Keep it up though, maybe your whimpering will draw them out."

"There's no light down there anymore."

I pointed into the darkness, barely able to see my own hand in front of me.

"Keep your eyes on the ground. My satchel must've been buried, but we should be able to see where it landed, since the floor is see-through."

About the time I said so, Loki's foot crushed a bubble, sending the sounds of shattering glass echoing through the darkness.

"I don't think there's enough light to see anything now Odin. At least before we had an angry fire giant to help out."

"What?" I said sarcastically, "you don't know any tricks that'll help us? Do you only know ones that cause trouble?"

"Matter of fact," Loki said, "now that you mention it, I think I do have a way to brighten things up a little: my shining personality."

"Oh, I thought that's what we were using already." I couldn't help but adding.

Loki laughed in the dim light coming from the distant mouth of the cave, the sun nearly set completely over the Eastern horizon.

"No, that's your dull personality. Here's mine; behold!" he said, dramatically bursting into flames.

The cave was filled with flickering golden-yellow light, which was reflected from the black glass on the floor, projecting what looked like a starry sky onto the cold stone of the ceiling.

"Thank you Loki; that's quite an effect, now keep looking" I said dismissively, resisting the urge to acknowledge what a beautiful thing Loki had done.

Loki was obviously amused by his work, and it was for that reason alone he had done it at all. He and I both knew this to be a fact and for that reason, I couldn't give him the attention he was after.[10]

"Don't you want to bask in the glory of my starry night, Odin?"

Keeping my eyes on the ground, trying not to encourage him, I said, "Yes, I do, and I am, but there is an important task at hand and accomplishing it under the light of your trickery only makes it harder. If I were not a god, I don't think finding my bag would be possible with such a distraction, now stay focused on the path ahead and stop wasting time with your eyes in the sky."

"But Odin," Loki said, pointing toward a constellation of lights, "don't you see that group of stars that looks like a fish?[11]

"Loki!" I yelled in frustration, momentarily glancing up at what the mischief-maker was pointing at, "I need you to focus. What's that?" I stopped mid-thought, pointing excitedly toward the fish constellation.

"It's a fish, that's what I said. Are you okay?"

"Not the lawful fish" I said, "the light next to it."

"It's a golden ring. How about that? I'm pretty talented after all. Looks like the fish is swimming around it."

"Are you messing with me, Loki?"

"Didn't I tell you I do pretty awesome things by accident all the time? I mean, I'm not even trying, but these things come so easy to me."

"It's not you at all fool." I said, fed up with his silliness. "The light's coming from one of the bubbles. See that shaft of light leading up to it?"

A golden beam led from the halo on the ceiling to a single black bubble several feet from where we stood. I quickly made my way toward it, getting down on my hands and knees. I placed my face close to the glassy dome, trying to see inside.

"What is it boy? What do you smell?" Loki said with a smile as he stood behind me.

The light in the cave became much more dim. I looked back over my shoulder momentarily and noticed that Loki had extinguished his flaming body until only his hair was alight.

Turning back to the translucent glass I spoke.

"I'm not sniffing anything Loki." My voice muffled with my mouth so close to the ground. "There's something here. It's hard to see."

I stood up, looking around the floor for a tool of some kind.

Unsuccessful, I stepped back, raised the heel of my boot, and slammed it down into the shining bubble.

"So much destruction from you Odin! Why do you always want to break things? I thought that was why you don't like giants."

As I knelt down, carefully picking out shards of glass from the hole I'd made, I answered Loki's question.

"You've got a point, but if you want to create something, you've got to destroy something else. It's the law, like a gift for a gift. There's always a trade-off. If you want to build a house," I flung a chunk of black glass over my shoulder, "you cut down some trees. If you want to eat, you kill a plant or animal and eat it."[12]

I looked up at Loki.

"So, you're saying you gads need us to break things so you've got something to fix?" he asked.

"No. There's a difference between destroying things with a purpose and doing it for fun. The trade-off has to be balanced. Destruction is the father of creation."

"So, what I think you're trying to say is that if it weren't for breaking things, nothing would ever get done."

"Yeah, I guess Loki. You really are dull sometimes."

"So," he continued, "I can still break things for fun sometimes, right?"

"No" I said pointedly before looking back into the hole. "Never."

I reached in and grabbed hold of something. I struggled to dislodge whatever it was, the muscles in my back straining with effort.

"What is it Odin? "Did you find your, I mean, my, pile of metal scraps? I hope so. I was getting so worried."

All at once the object came free and I nearly tumbled over backwards into Loki. I quickly regained my balance and simply sat on my haunches, marveling.

Loki stepped forward and peered down at what I now held.

Shining brightly, it was a silver and gold ring, as big around as a man's arm. The ring hummed a high note, like a bell which had been rung. The runes that had been engraved down the blade and upon the hilt of my old knife were now neatly spaced around the outside edge of the object. The two lustrous metals had swirled together into spirals of varying complexity, creating the sparkling light which had projected through the glass lens, onto the ceiling.

"How do you suppose that happened?" Loki said, "Seems weird.[13]

I couldn't help but softly chuckle.

"Yeah, Loki, it's weird alright. There was another bubble from before under this one. I think the knife melted around it and made a ring. I guess everything else, my bag included, burned away."

"I knew Stinger would become something new, something as useful, but I didn't expect this. There's no way this is a coincidence. It's not an accident."

"I don't know man, it could be, remember the fish and the ring? That was an accident."

"No, it wasn't. You didn't do that. The ring just happened."

"Wall," he said, "on purpose – accident – does it even really matter?"

"No, it doesn't, but we should make it matter either way" I said, not allowing him to distract me.[14]

"Back on the plain we keep a ring like this to swear oaths on. When people get married or make a deal, they both hold the ring and promise to keep it, last the oathbreaker suffer something bad."

"Seems silly to only keep a promise because you're being threatened if you don't. Maybe we should name the ring Hat Band, because it just holds your oath over your head" Loki observed.

"That's not why you keep a promise. You make an oath because you want to, and you keep it because that's the right thing to do. The ring is just the container where the promise is kept, so it doesn't disappear into the mists of memory. The only thing forcing you to keep your oath is your own sense of honor and if you've got no honor, you're probably already suffering, so breaking it wouldn't matter anyway."

I stood up, holding the ring out to Loki.

"You're my friend. I think you're an honorable person and that this ring was meant to stand for our friendship."

Loki looked at me like I was speaking a foreign language.

"What's wrong Loki?" I asked. "Do you disagree?"

"No" he said. "What's that noise? Sounds; like someone singing."

I felt the ring vibrating and realized the noise Loki had heard was coming from it.

"It's the ring. I guess some of Stinger's power is left in it, but it's different somehow."

"Well then, maybe we should name it Singer."

"Are you naming it then? What are you going to give for a naming gift?" I asked. "That's the tradition, right?"

"I don't know." Loki said, "What do you give a ring as a gift?"

"It is an oath ring. Maybe you should give an oath."

Loki, smiling playfully, reached for the ring and we both held it tightly.

"I swear upon this ring, Singer, to share my friendship with you, Odin of Ida Plain, and that we will remain friends until the end of time.[15]

I smiled warmly at this and gave my own oath upon the ring.

"I swear – my friendship to you, Loki of the Ironwood, and that I will never lift a horn in celebration unless you are there to celebrate with me."[16]

While we still held the ring, we crossed arms and shook hands over it to seal the deal.

Loki, never able to be serious for long quickly unclasped my hand and said "Now let's get out of this hole before something else happens. Between the etins and your blossoming sentiment, there's been too much already."

Loki was quick to take the lead, walking briskly back toward the caves entrance. I followed, fitting the ring on my upper arm for lack of a better place to keep it. The time had finally come for me to begin my journey home.

<u>Dagaz</u>

Night had come. The only light to be seen was emanating from Loki's flaming head and were it not for that, we wouldn't not have been able to find our way.

The cave's mouth came into view and Loki suddenly extinguished himself.

"What's that all about Loki? I can't see anything."

"Wouldn't want to attract undue attention from the forest, now, would we?" ha responded. "There are creatures out that we won't want to run into."

"I suppose you would know best", I agreed.

Outside, the wolf cubs waited for us patiently, and/ware obviously happy to be reunited with us when we appeared.

"See?" Loki pointed at the pups, "At least they had enough sense to stay out of harm's way."

I reached down and fumbled for the pups in the dark, scratching them both behind the ears.

"Yeah Loki, that's 'cause they are just hungry little monsters. A lot more is expected of us. It's probably better that I don't drag them with me into every situation and have them getting in the way or distracting me anyway."[2]

I gazed out into the distant darkness.

"I've been gone a long time. My family's probably wondering what's taking me so long. My method will be worried"

"Missing your mommy Odin?" Loki sniggered as he picked up a rock. "If you're in a hurry," he said, rearing his arm back to launch it, "we'd better be on our way."

He threw the piece of shale downhill, toward the forest canopy, with a laugh, rashly contradicting his earlier warning.

"You're in for a treat" he said as the stone flew.

"Why would you do that Loki!" I asked, shocked.

As the stone entered the canopy, the sounds of tearing leaves and snapping twigs were accompanied by howls and hisses. Yellow and red eyes appeared in pairs and soma standing alone, glaring from the limbs and from in between the trunks of trees.

"I would have preferred to go quietly and carefully, but since you're in such a hurry, we can take the more exciting route. Come on; it'll be fun."

I looked at him skeptically.

"What do you have in mind?"[3]

The fiery boy said nothing more before he just took off running, as he was wont to do, bounding downslope with a small avalanche of shale following him.

I had no choice but to follow again, the wolves fast at my heels.

As Loki neared the edge of the forest he began to catch fire. First, his feet, which left flaming footprints at every step, then his legs, spreading blue and orange flame toward his waist and flaring out behind him. His hands were ablaze, leaving tracers of light in bright arcs as they pumped at his sides.

I had to increase my distance from him to avoid being burned when he caught fire completely. Ribbons of flame stretched out between us, Geri and Freki fanned out wisely, one on either side of me.

I was completely unarmed and had to rely solely upon Loki's knowledge of the Ironwood and his ability to fend off whatever may lie within it.[4]

He ran Westward, back toward Ida Plain, but with a good distance, and at least one bottomless chasm, between us and that goal.

Loki's path was easy to see as his fiery footprints faded, giving me a clear and precise path to follow. I knew that if my feet fell in the exact places where Loki had stepped, as long as he was still standing, I would be too.

Loki's footprint flickered on a large stone, so I stepped there. Then, a flaming patch of earth, so there my foot fell. Upon a fallen log, then a twisted root.

Were it not for what lurked in the deep shadows created by his luminescence, the journey would have been as easy and as straightforward as a walk on the plain. His light turned out to be both a guide and a danger.

Our going went well until I began to feel something snagging my tattered and burned shirt. I ignored the first, slight tugs, hoping they were only tree limbs or vines, but when I clearly felt a clawed hand try to catch me by the shoulder, my hope for something so innocent vanished and was replaced with the readiness that comes before battle.[5]

My senses were on high alert as I noticed the glowing eyes along our winding path getting closer and closer.

"Your kinsmen are becoming more friendly Loki. I think they might want to eat me."

Loki didn't slow down as he laughed at me.

"Not just you my friend. They'd eat me too, family or not."

Right about the time Loki stopped his yapping, a large, sausage-fingered fist, reached from the darkness and snatched Freki from the safety of the light. The wolf cub yelped in fear.

Geri and I stopped immediately, but Loki continued on for several paces.

"Just leave him Odin, or we'll all suffer the same fate. He's just a mutt. You said so yourself."

"No!" I yelled at him in anger, "he may only be an animal, but he's as much my friend as you are."

Loki's light was dim where Geri and I stood, and the woodland creatures began closing in upon us. Crouched with my fist clenched tight, I prepared to fight and if necessary, tear limb from limb, whatever threatened my friends and I.

As the sounds of Freki's frightened cries grew further away, Geri, snarling, bolted into the darkness and now it was I who brought up the rear.

Loki, reluctantly, followed.

As Geri followed the trail of his lost brother by smell, the glowing eyes of the forest drew ever closer, until the weak light Loki offered was not enough to deter them any longer.

A small beast, all fur and teeth, jumped out of the shadows at Geri, only to be caught midair in the wolf's jaws and tossed back into the darkness. Geri never even slowed down.

Another large wight which looked like a shriveled old man with huge yellow eyes and see-through skin lunged at me. The light coming from Loki's waning mane shone through the goblin's large ears, revealing a web of green and blue veins. I effortlessly grasped the creature by these batwings and tossed him back from where he came.

"A goblin, Odin!" Loki exclaimed. "Don't see them everyday."

Loki finally closed the distance between us, but even so, he offered a weak source of light to stave off the monsters.

"Why don't you quit messing around and help us get our friend back, Loki?"

"What's that? The great Odin Borson needs my help?" Loki said, just to rub it in. "Why, certainly. I'll save you and your poor wolfling."

Loki exploded in a huge ball of fire, illuminating a horrifying crowd of night creatures gathered around us. From the roaring flames leapt an impressive, flaming mountain lion. His long tail swished back and forth for a moment before he dove ahead of Geri and I, batting the spooks away with the flick of his huge paws and quickly closing the gap between us and whatever had nabbed our missing companion.

The remaining wolf cub and I struggled to keep up, but the wake created by Loki's light and the fear he had stuck into the surrounding forest vermin cleared our path so that we were no longer continuously threatened.

Our war party made its way swiftly into the North and it became apparent to all that we were approaching the same, roaring river which we had left behind earlier in the day. I heard the sounds of the fast-flowing water in the distance clearly through the trees and stones. Loki repelled the wildlife of the forest and our travel remained fast and focused as we trailed our flaming feline friend, rarely having to defend ourselves.

As we made our way, I noticed that the same rune was carved into every large boulder we came upon. Between the quickly changing shadows and tree trunks, I could make out what appeared to be an hour glass on its side. The only ideas I could form about its meaning were muddled with the thought of returning to this stretch of forest, which I was certain I had seen earlier in the day. The place seemed to have changed somehow, though. The journey had come full circle and the magic of the standing stones was directing the path we were on.

Up ahead I heard the angry roar of the giant fire-cat and made my way coward the sound, close at the heels of Geri. The halo of light around Loki showed the edge of the river stretching out in both directions. Whatever Loki had been chasing was trapped and unable to cross the treacherous river rapids with its prey.

A large, dark form, rocked back and forth, holding its massive hands to its ugly face. Freki could hardly be seen, clutched in the creature's grip, near its slack and drooling jaw.

The beast looked like a mountain of loose flesh. Roll upon roll seemed to teeter on the edge of the river, as if about to topple and wash downstream. There was a dead, distant look in the giant's eyes, which suggested it was only barely able to comprehend what was happening. It clearly wanted only to feed itself, but could only do so with the least possible effort. Having co work for a meal was out of the question.[6]

The resistance Freki was offering as he fought and fiercely bit at the giant's hand, coupled with the determination of his friends, who had the giant surrounded, was far too much for a creature so accustomed to simply stuffing his face.

Loki crouched before the slothful mound of flesh, prepared to pounce. He slowly crept forward, his shoulder blades protruding from his flaming feline back. As he toyed with his prey, Geri and I closed in, one of us on each flank.

The monster shuffled backwards in fear. His heels sluggishly neared the rocky bank of the river, which fell away sharply into the rapids. Loki moved forward slowly, very slowly, before lunging with lightning speed. The giant moaned in sudden terror as he fell backwards into the water, throwing Freki into the air before him.

I dove to save my friend, barely catching him before, he too, was consumed by the torrential river. Loki landed nimbly at the water's edge, his flaming tail and his golden mane blazing brightly in the night. Gen ran to Freki and I and nipped joyfully at his litter-mate's fur. As I lay on the ground in a state of relief, both of the pups stood on my chest, licking at my face.

"Thank you Loki! You did it."

Loki morphed into his handsome human form and stood over us smiling his charismatic smile.

"I did, didn't I? I don't think I've ever had this much fun in my life. Say we'll do it again sometime Odin. Can't we?" he said, acting like an overjoyed young girl.

"I don't ever want to join you for anything like this again" I said, "Seems like you can have enough fun by yourself when you're in this mountain lion form."

"What do you mean by that?" Loki asked, pretending not to know the answer.

"Didn't you say you were familiar with the cat who left me that welcoming pile of poop this morning? I'm willing to bet, no, don't get me wrong, I know, you're very familiar with this cat, indeed."

I sat up, continuing to scratch and pet the wolves as I spoke.

"You're full of tricks and surprises Loki; some more welcomed that others."

Laughing, he offered his hand to help me to my feet.

"I guess that just comes naturally to me my friend." He pulled me upright.[7]

"I don't suppose I'd even be here for all of this if it wasn't for your own natural talents. I'm used to doing my own thing, and look at me now. I've been with you all day. You didn't force me here, did you?"

I had to think about this for a moment, ever leery of Loki's riddles.

"No, I didn't force you to follow me." I said, still unsure of his meaning.

"Well, what is it then?" Loki said.

"I can't say. Why do you think you're here?"

"You've got a powerful will my friend."

He clapped me on the back and pulled me by the shoulder, down the path in the direction of Ida Plain.

"I suppose that's because what you do is usually the right thing, it's hard to resist following."

As I walked, I thought deeply to myself.

"Sounds like I may be a lot more like my brothers than I thought."

The eyes in the darkness were beginning to take

notice of our little band once more.

"We'd better put a move on," Loki said, "lest we have to battle every varmint in the forest tonight."

The rest of his body ignited, illuminating the surrounding woods.

"Let's make an end to this adventure."

He began jogging, increasing his speed until he had us all running at full speed, once again, led by his flaming footprints.

"Not much farther now" I said aloud, finishing the thought silently, "seems the furthest edge of this wilderness was not in the direction Loki thought."

I finally realized that the real journey I had been on was into the, as of yet, unexplored depths of my own spirit.[8]

We ran, this time without so much resistance. It seemed the reckoning we had given the forest trolls was a good deferent to keep them at bay.

As we moved through the forest, our group became as one. It was obvious that these were Loki's places. He effortlessly ran the woodland path, bounding from rock to rock, from one root to the next. I was close at hand, retracing each of his steps as the flames left behind dwindled. The ring on my arm seemed to glow with an internal light, though, at the time, I hadn't noticed.[9]

The wolves, running by pure instinct, moved with a sureness and stealth which seemed to grow stronger with every passing minute. Their movements were closely synchronized with my own and the three of us became bound together by some invisible force.

From the shadows peered the glowing eyes of the forest, lighting the rock walls and standing stones so characteristic of the Ironwood. Only barely able to be seen by the likes of others besides myself, were dull runes, deeply carved and craftily placed, emanating from the darkness.

"Sparks fly from a struck flint; a yew tree stands tall, its roots descending to unknown depths; friends enjoy peace in one another's company, then, the harvest.[10]

I saw myself with my tribe. We were one.

"There will be much to learn" my mind shifted again, "come harvest, come Winter; not only from my family, but from the giants as well, and come Spring, from the Vanir."

The end of the journey seamed to fly by. The stones and trees of the day were not the same as before. All of them had been a blur that morning as well; I had been swept toward this unexpected transformation.

I paid close attention now, but still, for some reason could not see far enough ahead to know where exactly we were or how much further we had to go. I couldn't tell that we had come to the place where we had begun until my new friends and I had actually arrived.

Othala

The narrow chasm stretched out North and South, probably, somewhere, joining the void where Ymir still thrashed and tore at the worlds.

Loki slowed his pace as we approached until, finally, we were all walking; the flames of his body shrank until all that burned, once again, was his hair, and something else, something deep within his eyes. It may have been a reflection of my glowing arm ring, I theorized, Singer, Loki had named it, or it could have been something originating within him, his spirit perhaps.

I looked more closely as he stopped and turned toward us, feeling as if I were tumbling into those pools of flickering light. I saw myself within them.

"My reflection is all", I told myself, though I knew better.

I looked down at the wolf cubs. They peered back up at me. Their eyes, too, were clear and reflective, though they lacked that internal glow. I saw myself there as wall.

"What is this? What's happening?" I thought as Loki began to speak.

"Seems we've arrived my friend. Now I can't tell your smell from the smell of the countryside."

I shook my head in weary resignation. Loki had no regard for the state of awe I found myself in and couldn't pass up an opportunity to joke.

"Not my small after all, Loki. Next time you decide to take a dump, maybe pick a better place than right in the middle of the foot path. Never mind that though", I said. "Why do I feel so strange? What is this place? I feel like I'm waking from a dream."

Loki just shrugged.

"How should I know? Maybe you need a nap", he said dismissively.

I sensed that he knew more than he was letting on.

"This is where we part ways." Loki said as he offered his hand.

"Are you sure you don't want to visit my garth on

the plain? It's not nearly as exciting at the Ironwood, but it's got its pleasures. You might like it."

"No" Loki quickly responded, "not now. I've got some family business to see to." he lied. "Mom and Dad are getting together and I don't want to miss the fireworks."[2]

I accepted his cryptic answer, aware of his evasion.

"I can't imagine what your parents must be like, considering your personality. They must be pretty interesting."

I paused and an uncomfortable silence ensued. In an effort to break it, I changed the subject.

"Well, the night is almost over. I might make it home before Sunna rises. I'll come back. Do you think I'll see you again?" I asked as I shook Loki's hand.

"See that ring on your arm?"

We both stared at the mysteriously glowing treasure.

"So" I said, "I guess you're going to want it now that it's not a jumble of scrap metal?"

"No, friend, there's a promise within it that

belongs to both of us. I think that will draw us together, if nothing else. One way or another we're going to run into each other again, of that, I'm sure. So, when you return, that's when you can give it to me. We'll share it. It'll give us a reason to seek each other out."

I smiled.

"Why do you think it's glowing?" I asked.

"Did you get any of that giant's drool on it?" he said with a smirk.

"I think it's got something to do with our oath." I said, ignoring him entirely. "There's power in it now. It's bright enough to light my way through the rest of the forest. I'll consider that a gift from you, since you've done so wall at it 'til now."

I looked down at the wolves.

"You two have done your fair share as well. Greedy and single-minded though you might be, you've proven faithful friends. I don't suppose either of you would want to leave your home either."

I squatted down and ruffled the fur of each wolf in turn. They returned the affection, sniffing and licking at my hands.

Standing, I looked over the chasm and noticed the

same rock which had been engraved with a thorn earlier in the day, was now marked differently. I squinted in the darkness. The new rune was emanating a weak light which was barely able to be seen, but it whispered to me "home".

"Home" I heard from within myself.

"Do you hear that Loki?" I asked, knowing full well he had.

A short silence was broken with "Whee-eep. Pfff." as Loki farted quietly.

"I do. I do, Odin." he said in a reverent tone. "What does it mean?"

I shook my head in disgust, an irresistible smile stretching across my face. Then, both of us broke out in laughter. We laughed for several minutes and when we were finally able to catch our breath, I held out my hand again.

Loki met it. I pulled him in close and clapped him on the back before letting go completely, turning and running toward the breach which separated his chaotic world from my own, more orderly land.

As I bounded toward the divide, Geri and Freki whimpered excitedly at the sight of my sudden departure. I would later discover they had both taken off after me as soon as I neared the edge, ignorant of the breadth of the gorge.

At the time, I didn't know they were following me, but even as Loki watched what was happening, he did nothing to prevent this tragedy from unfolding.

I ran toward the gap, three quick steps to get my speed up; three more long paces to gather my momentum and three final, bounding strides before leaping into the air over a certain death, should I come up short.[3]

I was a powerful boy. As I flew through the air, Geri and Freki neared the edge of the rock from which I had just jumped, about to follow me across this uncertain span. Loki waited until the last possible moment before intervening.

With lightning speed, he stepped forward. Had time been dramatically slowed, his movement would have seemed casual and lackadaisical, but in real time, he was so swift he became a blur, streaking toward the edge.

Just as they left the ground, Loki caught them both by the scruff of their necks in midair. Their bodies curled up as their backsides swung out over the emptiness, before Loki yanked them back to safety.

"Not quite strong enough to make that leap on

your own, friends." he said as he held them up to his face.

I landed squarely upon the same stone I had leapt from that morning. After gaining my bearings, I turned for one more farewell when I took notice of Loki and the pups.

"What're you doing, Loki?"

Ha calmly replied, "Oh, I figured since you were gone, I could toss these two down to Hel to see how far it is."

He began to crack a smile.

Squinting in comprehension, knowing Loki well enough to tell when he was lying, I couldn't help but laugh.

"Did they try to make the jump?"

"Yes" Loki laughed with me, "the mutts were going to kill themselves to be with you; greedy 'till the end."

"Mindless creatures" I said, shaking my head, "but you've got to love them. I suppose you could toss them over one by one, since they seem to want to come along so badly."

Loki made as if he was going to punt Freki over the breach, but instead laughed again before swinging the wolf underhanded, releasing him into flight. The pup, still balled up, flew into my arms. In quick succession, the trickster tossed the second wolf, who was caught with equal dexterity.

I sat the puppies down and scratched them fondly.[4]

"So, it seems you may discover a life of a different sort after all. There'll be plenty for you to eat where I'm taking you, I'm sure."

I stood straight and looked back to Loki. Waving goodbye, I yelled to him, "farewell my friend, the fourth and fairest. Fare your forth, to find your fellows."

Loki smiled and waved back, responding in like.

"Not far we friends must fare to find them, when our fellows fare forth freely."

He broke from versa. "Come back and see me soon my friend."

With that, Loki, the fiery haired boy from the forest, turned and transformed himself into a large mountain lion, a form he was clearly fond of. I watched him until I noticed him drop his hindquarters, hunch his back and prepare to relieve himself right there, on the doorstep of the Ironwood.

Trying to avoid this sight, I turned my gaze quickly to the West, the glow of the oath ring on my arm illuminating the standing stone at the chasm. The rune on it was now much easier to see. It showed me rolling green hills and verdant swaths of land, dotted with barley. It showed me beautiful rings of standing stones, still grouped together symmetrically, as they had been for unknown ages. I saw the familiar walls of my garth and smoke rising from the roof of my humble home.

I was lost in memories of Ida Plain for a moment before my mind was unexpectedly drawn toward memories more recent. The daylight; the thorn on this very rock; the tumble I had taken, then the dream I had while I was knocked out: lightning in the clear blue sky; the blazing forest fire.

"What did it mean?" I asked myself.

My sharp mind sifted through all I had learned. The pieces slowly began to come together.

Loki's words throughout the previous day rang in my head: "He only shows up when there's a storm brewing... My father struck this rock... Fireworks...." Than lighting flashed in my mind again.

"The fire," I thought. "The trees."

Loki's most significant characteristics became one.

I yelled for my friend before I turned around, "Loki!", only to discover he was already gone. I could still see a small flame through the trees in the distance. "Loki!" I yelled again. "I know who you are! I know who your parents are!" but he did not respond.

In the distance Loki surely heard me calling, heard my words, but ignored me. I only he hoped he knew why his parentage even mattered to me.

To myself I whispered "we are who we are after all, but true friends will be friends ever." then I saw Loki's flames extinguish as he joined his fallows in the darkness of the nighttime forest.

I saw the tiny flame disappear, leaving me alone with the only light to be seen in those deep woods.

The wolf cubs whined softly.

"Let's go then", I said to them before stepping from the fallen stone. "We've still got quite a journey to make before we can say we're home."

We walked, then ran, our path able to be seen wall enough, though I could have run this one in the dark. This was a well trod way that I'd gone before, many times, and though it didn't lead to the same thrilling sense of discovery, it did lead me toward another sense I had failed to recognize before.

I longed now for the warmth of the hearth fire and to hear the chatter of my family gathered at the table.

I followed the trail I had worn in the forest floor, the wolf cubs close at heal. As I made my way toward the Western edge of the forest, the canopy began to open up, giving me a glimpse of the starry sky. Though the stars in those days, the morning of time, didn't yet hang in any given place, they still provided us a respite from the darkness. I understood this as a sign of journey's end.

As I drew closer to the plain, even the brightness of the moon shone through the tree tops. It hung full in the sky, rolling along like a rock who had yet to find its own path to tread.

My eyes adjusted to the light and where the shadows and depths of the night hadn't seemed so dark before, they became all the more forbidding. The huge roots I clambered over seamed to writhe in the shifting light. The small stone cliffs we climbed over held their own pools of blackness against themselves greedily.

I paid them little mind. I was almost name and it was there my mind and memory were out to scout.[5] My vision flew out before me and brought back word of what I now longed for: the bonds of family; something even stronger than friendship, though no less important.

As the final wall of giant trees appeared and I could see the plain beyond, I slowed my pace. I thought of my intent at the beginning of this journey, to find the outer edge of the Ironwood, and realized that I had done much more. I had found the edge of the entire world, and this world was not nearly the place I had once believed it to be.

The bounds of my realm ware not so distant as I had imagined, and beyond, a force to be reckoned with.

"Ymir will be brought low" I told myself with surety, "but I can't do it alone. Not even Loki, if he would help, would be enough. I will have to speak to my brothers about it. They'll understand."

I stood between two trees, looking out upon the open grassland. The distant horizon was still dark blue, but the light elves were at play, reaching their rosy fingers into the West.[6]

Weariness swept over me. I'd been going for a long time by then. I looked forward to some much-needed rest.

Stepping from beneath the arbor of the Ironwood, I felt as if I were finally waking up, in spite of my strong desire for sleep. A groggy, fogginess behind my eyes was lifted and my surroundings became more clear than they had ever been before.

I could see the green of the grass. I could near the soft breeze through the barley. I smelled the earth and the freshness of Summer. As I padded across the turf, the sun continued to rise, the sky growing brighter, with a mixture of blues, purples and pinks. I saw my garth at the top of a rising hillock and couldn't help but pick up my pace.

The last rune I saw at the chasm was lingering in my mind, drawing me closer to home, making me appreciate what that meant.

Perthro

His head lulled as he slept, still sitting at the table.

"Wode." his wife said, "why don't you go for a walk or something. You've been at the table for far too long."

"Yes, Frea, yes. I think I will." he said before he is distracted again, startled by a distant laughing. A laugh he knows all too well.

"Loki?" he whispers. "What have you done?"

He looks to the roost atop his high seat, where are perched two ravens.

"Hugin, awake! Munin? Fly out over the worlds to Niflhel. I fear the time has come."[2]

The ravens fly out of the hall through the opened door.

"What is it Wode? What's happening?" his wife asks.

"The battle is at hand my love. Loki has been freed. Prepare yourself."

Frigga looks at her husband with a fierceness in her eyes which betrays her motherly bearing.

"I knew, Wode. I just didn't want to say anything. I'm ready."[3]

Her hands ball into fists and Odin smiles to himself at his wife's strength.

"Geri? Freki? You've got another battle in you too, don't you?"

Both of the huge wolves howl their agreement in unison.

"My hat Frigga, bring my spear, I've got to..."

Odin's commands are interrupted by the blaring of a battle horn, so loud it rocks the walls of

Valhalla.[4]

"There's Heimdall. It's closer than I thought. I've got to talk to her again. I've got to see the Vala."[5]

At that, Odin silently leaves the hall and in only a moment is seen riding his eight-legged steed away into the East. The sun barely hangs above the western horizon, casting its fiery red light down his path, before sinking, finally, beyond the twighlight.[6]

Footnotes

*<u>On Loki's Side</u> refers to the unconscious mind, which, here, would be Loki's home, or his 'side' of the chasm.

Opening

1) Ida Plain, here, is representative of the surface of awareness, or consciousness. (Voluspa 7, Hollander)

Opening

2) "A little lake-hath but little sand:/ but small the mind of man;/ not all men are – equally wise,/ each wight wanteth somewhat." (Havamal 53, Hollander)

Raidho

1) Raidho – Signifies the beginning of Odin's spiritual journey. (Old English Rune Poem – "Riding is in the hall – to every warrior/ easy, but very hard – for the one who sits up/ on a powerful horse – over miles of road.")

2) Odin, Vili & Ve are three parts of a single psyche. Odin is inspiration, Vili is will and Ve is wonder, or a sense of Awe. At the mundane level of consciousness the differences and similarities between them are taken for granted.

3) The standing stones throughout the story, and especially here, are allusions to the ambiguous verse 2 in Voluspa, possibly suggesting previous iterations of the World Tree in multiple cycles of life and subsequent destruction.

4) "...beware thou of – bandying words/ with an unwise oaf,/ For from evil man – not ever wilt thou/ get reward for good;/...." (Havamal 122-123, Hollander)

5) After the slaying of Ymir, the sky will be filled with clouds made from Ymir's brains, or Brow (Gylfaginning 8, Grimnismal 42)

6) The Ironwood is the wilderness of Norse myth, hone to Fenris's offspring. Here, in essence, it's Jotunheim, or the unconscious (Lokasenna 42, Volundarkvida open prose 1,3,5,7 & 14)

7) "...the sun knew not – what seat [s]he had,/ the stars knew not – what stead they held,/ the moon knew not – what might the] had." (Voluspa 5, Hollander)

8) The giants, too, are aspects of the psyche, though here a conflict arises and the psyche is resistant to their presence. The forces of order are the counter-balance in the entropic system, making Odin the exception to the rule, rather than the other way around. For every one part of order, there must be two parts of chaos. Mind is only a

beacon in the field of consciousness.

9) This is the commencement of Odin's tireless pursuit of knowledge, first exploring his own psychic cosmos.

10) Wode, or Odr, is the root of Odin's name and is representative of inspiration, will power and ecstasy; all three brothers – Odin, Vili & Ve.

11) The familiar portion of the Ironwood, here, represents the Personal Unconscious and the Working Memory, easily available to recall.

<u>Thurisaz</u>

1) Thurisaz – Signifies the unconscious realm of the archetypes and Id. (Tile Old Icelandic Rune Poem – "Thurs is the torment of women and the dweller in the rocks and the husband of the etin-wife varth-runa. Saturn, "ruler of the legal assembly")

2) At this point in the lore Odin hasn't yet 'won' the runes, so he had to intuit their meanings upon exposure.

3) The chasm is the boundary between the Personal Unconscious and the Collective Unconscious.

4) Thurisaz – (Old English Rune Poem – "Thorn is very sharp; – for every thegn/ who grasps it/ it

is harmful – and exceedingly cruel/ to every man – who lies upon it.)

5) An example of the strategic mentality of Odin's spirit.

6) This is the emergence of Loki, as the Shadow Self, from Odin's Self and Ego.

7) This illustration is a simile for Ragnarok, Loki's part in it, and Odin's attitude towards its inevitability. (Voluspa 56, Hollander)

8) Once Odin crosses the threshold, his Shadow is separated from him and Loki appears as an individual.

9) Loki's parents, according to Our Father's Godsaga ch.12, are Laufey – Tree Top, and Farbauti – Errant Lightning.

10) Ymir, as stasis and disorder, is used by Odin, hare, as an excuse for the poor state of things in the cosmos and an object of blame, instead of a motive for action and the substance of creativity.

11) Odin fails to recognize that he Loki are two sides of the same coin.

12) (The author is aware that the dwarves didn't yet exist before the slaying of Ymir, according to Gylfaginning 14, where they were like maggots in his flesh, but play along for the sake of the story).

13) Loki arbitrarily feigns ineptitude – because that's what tricksters do. Odin reacts inappropriately by mocking him. "A wise man he – who hies him betimes/ from the man who likes to mock;/ for at table who teases – can never tell/ what foe he might have to fight." (Havamal 31, Hollander)

14) Loki intentionally destroys Odin's Knife "...if ill thou trustest one,/ and hollow-hearted his speech:/ thou shalt laugh with him – and lure him on,/ and let him have tit for tat." (Havamal 46, Hollander)

15) In this case the number S foreshadows a cycle of life, death and rebirth.

Wunjo

1) Wunjo – this rune signifies the building friendship between Odin and Loki. (Old English Rune Poem – "Joy is had by the one who knows few troubles, pains or sorrows, and to him who himself has power and blessedness, and also the plenty of towns.")

2) Hagalaz – Creation/Destruction (Old English Rune Poem – "Hail is the whitest of grains, it comes from high in heaven, a shower of wind hurls it, then it turns to water.")

3) "So, well may it be" is a translation of the

Sanskrit word Swastika (Su-astika), according to Joseph Campbell, in his book Flight of the Mild Gander. The swastika is also represented hare by the sun's swirling light through the tree tops.

4) Odin is coming to terms with the presence of the character traits of the giants and his brothers within himself, integrating his shadow. "The ill-minded man – who meanly thinks,/ fleers at both foul and fair;/ he does not know, – as know he ought,/ that he is not free from flaws." (Havamal 22, Hollander)

5) This is the mirror image of Odin's perseverance against Ragnarok and a sign of Loki's lack of Odr, or Wode.

6) This sort of wager will end up causing trouble for Loki and the gods later in the lore (Skaldskaparmal 35, Our Father's Godsaga ch.23). Usually the wagers are proposed by dwarves & giants, indicating lower-level consciousness impulsive behavior – although the gods often participate.

7) Odin places great value upon the maegin in his knife, whether broken, or not. The lower order consciousness is unable to recognize this type of abstract value, it being a force one projects through identifying with an object.

8) This allusion isn't revisited, but refers to Loki's

role in Ragnarok, as mentioned in Voluspa 49-50, and indicates that by Loki's foreknowledge of it, he is perpetually duplicitous throughout the lore.

9) In several myths Odin is said to have done things he comes to regret and that he's criticized for, such as in Havamal 107-110: "...how put trust in his troth?", having broken his oath to Gunnlod.

10) Odin second guesses himself because he realizes, his greed for material belongings, and gluttony for victory have undermined his integrity. These negative character traits are substantiated into the characters, Geri and) Freki, and Odin doesn't hesitate to habituate them and come to terms.

11) Naturally Greed and Gluttony are self-interested, exhibiting a greed for life and personal safety.

12) Although Odin doesn't yet realize it, he no longer hungers for food after separating these flaws from himself and making them manageable. Odin lives by wine alone, mentioned in Grimnismal 19 and Gylfaginning 38.

13) Loki, as Odin's Shadow, reveals to him things about himself he wasn't yet aware of. The Shadow isn't the 'bad guy'; he's just a negative image.

14) The tradition of being obligated to provide a naming gift is illustrated in the legend of the naming of the Longobards, in which, having inadvertently named a tribe/army for their long beards, Odin is goaded by Frigga into giving them victory as well. (**I'm not sure where to find that story**)Fill in the blank.

15) Of course, we bury our biggest monsters the deepest in the unconscious.

16) Although Loki's loyalty is flimsy, Odin has determined to carry these psychic foibles at his own expense, so long as they play nice and continue to serve a practical purpose. In Grimnismal 19 Geri & Freki are said to feed on the flesh of the fallen in battle, allowing Odin to remain focused on the endgame – Odin drinks the wine of wisdom, which is strategy, in this case.

Elhaz

1) Elhaz – Offensive weaponry, Spiritual connection. This, in reference to Odin's desire to destroy Ymir, the making of the spear and the awareness of the spirit of the rock – the land wight. (The Old English Rune Poem – "Elk's sedge has its home – most of ten in the fen,/ it waxes in the water – and grimly wounds/ and burns with blood – any bairn/ who in any way – tries to grasp it.")

2) The name of Ymir is translated by Hollander, from Voluspa 3, as 'The Roarer'.

3) The repressions of the unconscious aren't as distant and disconnected as we'd like to believe. They're present in our daily thought processes, though only as undercurrents.

4) The unconscious is privy to information the conscious is unaware of. In this case, Odin had yet to travel very far outside his frame of reference.

5) Obviously, this is an allusion to the Slaying of Ymir and the ordering of the cosmos by Odin, Vili and Ve.

6) Ginnungagap is referred to in Voluspa 3 as 'a gaping nothing', and in Gylfaginning 5 as 'a yawning void'

7) Sowilo – here, more resembles the rune's shape as lightning than its meaning, as sunlight and is a reference to Loki's father Farbauti – (The Old Icelandic Rune Poem – "Sun is the shield of the clouds and shining glory and the lifelong sorrow of ice. Wheel. 'Descendant of the victorious one'.")

8) Our, genetic/psychic, heritage, is active in us whether we recognize it, or not, although a denial of it results in cognitive dissonance and discontent.

9) This scene is a rational illustration of animism and the landvettir. The idea is that not all spiritually active objects are self-aware and ego-centered.

10) All of the runic mysteries are universal aspects of reality. They're not the exclusive property of the Norse psyche. Only the symbols that represent them belong to the European folk, the forces themselves effect everybody.

11) Loki isn't the 'Devil', as some might characterize him. He has a purpose in the psychic cosmos, otherwise he wouldn't 'exist'. Odin doesn't discriminate on where he acquires wisdom from. He was criticized as unmanly for his practice of seithr (**Can't recall where to find that**). Fill in the blank.

12) One of the attributes of Odinic inspiration is the ability to improve upon preexisting ideas. Hare, Odin improvises a proto-Gungnir. The historical development of the stone spear could be seen as a sign of the emergence of Odinic spirituality in man. (Gungnir; Gylfaginning 51)

13) Odin's ever-present, and mounting anger is the next force to be integrated. At this point it begins to surface into the dreamscape.

Hagalaz

1) Hagalaz – Creation/Destruction, in reference to the impending integration of Odin's anger.

2) Odin is now able to reflect on the similarities between himself and his brothers, as opposed to the differences he was focused upon at the start.

3) Odin is 'thirsty' for wisdom. He drinks Odrerir in Havamal 107 &140, and in Gylfaginning he drinks from Mimir's well, out of the Gjallarhorn. Psychologically speaking, this wisdom is self-knowledge and expanded consciousness.

5) Although it wasn't Loki's intention, the opportunity to do something noble, for Odin, was a valuable gift. Havamal 76 says, because "...fair fame – will fade never,/ I ween, for him who wins it." Also, the act of accepting a gift graciously and without protest is as much a part of gifting as giving.

6) This scene is another mini Ragnarok, in which Odin is indifferent to death in order to complete what he's set out to do, which was determined when the 'dragon' went on the offensive.

7) "Holy Cow" seemed like a likely expression for this setting, referring to Audhumla, the Cosmic Cow, from Gylfaginning 6, who nourished Ymir.

8) Odin's anger substantiates itself and now he

must either face it, or run. The fire giant here resembles Surt, from Voluspa 51, and Skaldskaparmal 1,3 & 80, the giant who burns the World Tree, which could be interpreted as a similar threat of destruction to the psyche.

9) Odin throwing the spear over Loki's head is a symbolic sacrifice, as in Voluspa 24 when he does likewise over the Vanir. Here is means he has subordinated his Shadow to a higher cause.

10) Although we should tolerate character flaws in others, we shouldn't encourage them. Odin is putting into practice what he's learned about Loki and himself. Havamal 22 also applies here.

11) This is a vague reference to Andvari's Gold, which is associated with Sigurd's dragon slaying. (Reginsmal & Fafnismal)

12) A summary of the entropy represented by the gods & giants, and many other mythological symbols, such as the swastika and the triskel, which suggest that all is well in spite of the presence of 'bad' and destruction.

13) Weird is an English corruption of Wyrd, from the Indo European 'Wer– : to turn, or bend'.

14) Although the randomness of the universe and life is without purpose, we have the ability to provide purpose through the exercise of

consciousness. The universe doesn't 'do' things to us for a reason/ but we can use the things that happen to gain in wisdom and strength.

15) Loki's vow here, later broken, only compounds his regret, which turns to malice, exacerbating the torment he suffers until Ragnarok, described in Gylfaginning 50. This is the threat of failing to integrate the Shadow, with its resulting deterioration and disharmony.

16) This is a reference to Lokasenna 9. "Art mindful, Othin, – how in olden days we/ blended our blood together?/ Thou said'st that not ever – thou ale would'st drink/ but to us both it were born." (Hollander)

Dagaz

1) Dagaz – Day & Night in completion. This chapter is a return to the beginning. (The Old Norwegian Rune Poem – "Day is the lord's messenger – dear to men,/ the ruler's famous light; – (it is) mirth and hope/ to rich and poor – (and) is useful to all.")

2) The absence of greed and gluttony from Odin's motives are what allowed him to integrate his flaws successfully in the previous scene.

3) This is the beginning of the 'harried flight' of the Hero's Journey – one option provided for in

Campbell's observed structure.

4) Having integrated his Shadow – in the person of Loki – Odin could now rely upon Loki's knowledge of the unconscious as a guide through its perceived dangers with confidence.

5) The whole ecosystem of unintegrated psychic, ghouls attempt to impede Odin's effort to actualize the improved upon Self as he brings back what's been gained from the depths, into the realm of everyday awareness.

6) Sloth (laziness) attempts to usurp the prize – Odin's harnessing of gluttony – and reincorporate it into the unconscious. Laziness is a real threat to any effort to actualize the wisdom we're exposed to.

7) Odin & Loki – Ego & Shadow, both have individual characteristics which accentuate one another when they're integrated into a coherent Self.

8) The 'far edge' of this wilderness is journey's end and not some distant point in space. We don't 'go' anywhere in a spiritual journey of this kind.

9) This is a mirror image of the inbound journey and a waking from the trance-state represented by Odin's name as ecstasy.

10) The runes – Kenaz, Eihwaz,, Wunjo & Jera –

are intuited, but not fully understood by Odin as he wakes.

Othala

1) Othala – Homelands. As Odin returns to waking life, he comes to accept what is innate within himself (The Old Norwegian Rune Poem – "Estate is very dear – to every man,/ if he can enjoy what is right – and according to custom/ in his dwelling, – most often in prosperity.")

2) The 'fireworks' would be between Treetop and Errant lightning.

3) Nine steps, here, is a number of completion, bringing Odin full circle. This echoes Thor's nine steps in killing Jormungandr (Voluspa 55)

4) Odin brings these psychic foibles into his consciousness naturally, as opposed to forcing a disingenuous pretense, as is seen in many a zealous religionist.

5) This refers to the future emergence of Hugin and Munin, Odin's Ravens – 'Mind & Memory'. Grimnismal 20 "The whole earth over, – every day,/ hover Hugin and Munin;/ I dread lest Hugin – droop in his flight,/ yet I fear me still more for munin." (Hollander)

6) The play of the rising sun on the morning sky, here, is an allusion to the displays of the light

alfar.

Perthro

1) Perthro – Lot cup. Wyrd – the way things turn out as a result of what has happened in the past. (The Old English Rune Poem – "Lotbox is always – play and laughter/ among bold man – where the warriors sit/ in the beer-hall – happy together.")

2) Loki's laugh signifies that he has been freed from his bonds in Niflhel and that Ragnarok, the Twilight of the Gods', as opposed to the 'Morning of time', has finally come.

3) Frigga knows the future but doesn't tell it; living in stoic acceptance and readiness, as mentioned in Lokasenna 29 "...I ween that Frigg – the fates knoweth,/ though she say it not herself." (Hollander) The archetype of the Mother exists within both men and woman. Frigga represents, here, the ideal of the European Anima, in men, and something to emulate for women.

4) Gjallarhorn signals the affirmative end of the cycle, as told in Gylfaginning 27. Heimdall is the guardian of the bridge between the Ego-level consciousness and the realm of the Superego, and so his horn could represent a completion of the integration process, finally reaching equilibrium, or enlightenment.

5) This is the seeress from Voluspa. Odin never ceases to desire more wisdom from beyond his frame of reference, even at the end of time.

6) The sun now sets in the West, Odin having ordered the cosmos, although we can't ignore the fact that by him doing so he sets into motion this inevitable end. While the sun didn't know her path, there was no time and therefore there could be no 'end'. By setting out on a spiritual journey we expose ourselves to ugly truths we may wish we could forget. Havamal 55 says "Middling wise – every man should be:/ beware of being too wise;/ for wise man's heart – is happy seldom,/ if too great the wisdom he won." (Hollander)

Experts from: The Poetic Edda, Translated by Lee M. Hollander. University of Texas Press, Austin Tx, 1962

The Prose Edda: Tales from Norse Mythology, Snorri Sturlusson, Translated by Arthur Gilchrist Brodeur. Dover Publications Inc. Mineola, New York, 2006.

Printed in Great Britain
by Amazon

87826084R10091